She'd had en...

When she tried to step away, those fingers gripped the curve of her flesh tight, branding her. Tilting his head down, Mr. Ricci studied her, a mocking slant to his mouth. "Such outrage is not warranted, Ms. Fischer. Remember, you're only *pretending* to be mine."

Sam shivered as his words trickled down her spine like a lover's caress. She placed her palm on his chest, goaded beyond common sense. He was hard and hot against her fingertips. His heart thundering away belied the mockery in his eyes. "You wish I was yours. I do have standards."

His laughter enveloped her, a deep, sensual rumble, as arousing as the man's physicality. This close, she could see the warming of the gray of his eyes. The small scar across his brow. The flare of interest as he said, "And what are those?"

Tara Pammi can't remember a moment when she wasn't lost in a book—especially a romance, which was much more exciting than a mathematics textbook at school. Years later, Tara's wild imagination and love for the written word revealed what she really wanted to do. Now she pairs alpha males who think they know everything with strong women who knock that theory and them off their feet!

Books by Tara Pammi

Harlequin Presents

Fiancée for the Cameras
Contractually Wed
Her Twin Secret
Vows to a King
His Forgotten Wife
Baby Before Vows

Billion-Dollar Fairy Tales

Marriage Bargain with Her Brazilian Boss
The Reason for His Wife's Return
An Innocent's Deal with the Devil

The Powerful Skalas Twins

Saying "I Do" to the Wrong Greek
Twins to Tame Him

Visit the Author Profile page
at Harlequin.com for more titles.

ITALIAN'S LAST-MINUTE MISTRESS

TARA PAMMI

PRESENTS

If you purchased this book without a cover you should be aware that this book is stolen property. It was reported as "unsold and destroyed" to the publisher, and neither the author nor the publisher has received any payment for this "stripped book."

ISBN-13: 978-1-335-21369-3

Italian's Last-Minute Mistress

Copyright © 2026 by Tara Pammi

All rights reserved. No part of this book may be used or reproduced in any manner whatsoever without written permission.

Without limiting the exclusive rights of any author, contributor or the publisher of this publication, any unauthorized use of this publication to train generative artificial intelligence (AI) technologies is expressly prohibited. Harlequin also exercises their rights under Article 4(3) of the Digital Single Market Directive 2019/790 and expressly reserves this publication from the text and data mining exception.

This is a work of fiction. Names, characters, places and incidents are either the product of the author's imagination or are used fictitiously. Any resemblance to actual persons, living or dead, businesses, companies, events or locales is entirely coincidental.

For questions and comments about the quality of this book, please contact us at CustomerService@Harlequin.com.

TM and ® are trademarks of Harlequin Enterprises ULC.

Harlequin Enterprises ULC
22 Adelaide St. West, 41st Floor
Toronto, Ontario M5H 4E3, Canada
www.Harlequin.com

HarperCollins Publishers
Macken House, 39/40 Mayor Street Upper,
Dublin 1, D01 C9W8, Ireland
www.HarperCollins.com

Printed in Lithuania

ITALIAN'S
LAST-MINUTE MISTRESS

CHAPTER ONE

SAMEERA FISCHER STOOD in front of the wide marble steps at the entrance to the most beautiful villa on the shores of Lake Como and tried not to hyperventilate.

It was the first time she'd flown across the Atlantic. The first time she'd hopped on a plane to anywhere. The first time she wasn't accompanied by her overprotective parents.

That she'd traveled so far to meet a close friend/ex-boyfriend who had ghosted her for months couldn't muddy her satisfaction at what she had achieved.

Although it was alarming how much Matteo had hidden about his family's standing. Even she, a naïve twenty-three-year-old who'd never left San Francisco before, could tell that the property in front of her would be worth millions, if not more.

The villa shone against the black night, like the lake shimmering behind her, full of magnificent splendor, with the snow-tipped Alps a shadowy outline. The swarm of the designer-wearing crowd and the giant marquee on the grounds said she'd arrived right in the middle of a big-ass party.

Matteo, on one of his visits to San Francisco, had shown her pics, but only bits and pieces. The gardens that he adored but not the lake they led into. His bike but not the bright red Ferrari parked next to it. The view of Lake Como but not the spot where he'd stood when he'd taken the pic.

From the moment she'd boarded the flight to Milan—on a first-class flight and, then the chauffeured ride to Lake Como—an unsettling realization dawned. Matteo was no lowly manager in the rungs of Ricci International Finances as he'd claimed. Perhaps the fact that his surname was Ricci should have been a clue, but she'd never had reason to believe he'd lie to her...

Her confusion at his ghosting her only deepened.

Four months ago, they'd argued bitterly. No longer eighteen as when they'd met, Sam had realized that their relationship had run its course. Matteo would always remain her first boyfriend and a kind friend who had loved her during a hard time, yet they had nothing in common.

That she'd disappointed him by ending their relationship—after his patience over their long-distance relationship for nearly five years—saddened her. So surprising him by coming here had felt like a great idea. She knew that there was a friendship between them worth saving, even if the relationship was over, and this sudden silence from him worried her because it was so out of character.

Now as she stared at the glittering party, doubts engulfed her. Should she quietly leave? Wait for Matteo to show up in San Francisco again? Would he even come back, after ghosting her?

No, she couldn't give up now. Not on their friendship, not on herself.

This could be the summer where she experienced the world as a normal twenty-three-year-old. One summer where she didn't have to live with the crushing guilt that she'd ruined her parents' life.

One summer where she was bold, adventurous and daring.

Alessandro Ricci stared out of his bedroom window at his family's villa at the teeming guests and felt a spark of shame. He was the older son, and yet, he was avoiding extended family, important guests, the Bianchis among them and his aunt's extravagant emotions.

The last was what he needed escape from the most. It wasn't enough for his aunt that her son Matteo, Alessandro's half brother, was finally settling down. Oh no, his aunt who had raised Alessandro ever since his mother had died giving birth to him was now bemoaning Alessandro's own single status.

Since she was the one person in the entire world he loved more than anything, he hadn't snarled at her. Instead, he'd chosen to hide.

His presence cast a dark pall at these parties anyway. Especially when it was his thoroughly spoiled, good-for-nothing half brother Matteo's engagement party to the billionaire Bianchi heiress that Alessandro had had to engineer as if he were a bloody pimp. Not that he didn't appreciate the billion-dollar investment it brought to Ricci Finances.

Even after all these years, the gathering today reminded him of his own engagement party eighteen years ago. Of how incredibly happy he had been. How gloriously beautiful Violetta had looked. How arrogantly confident he'd been in his own power that the world was his for the taking.

In the months after he'd lost Violetta, he had hated others' happiness with a violent resentment, like a wounded feral animal. He'd hated the pity and concern, as if they were afraid for him and of him. The next few years, he'd thrown himself into sex with women who knew the score. But the short shelf life of his partners had only encouraged the young women and their mamas in his circle to portray him as a tormented man who needed to be saved by love.

Soon, the isolation had become his armor.

But in the last few months, even his father, a man of few words, had cast him concerned glances. Had started talking about how lost and broken he'd been after Alessandro's mother had died after giving birth to him. That he had saved himself by marrying his wife's younger sister, Maria.

His father didn't know it was too late for Alessandro.

Every day he'd stayed by Violetta's side as she'd tried, and failed, to fight the insidious cancer that had siphoned everything soft and good from him too. Every minute he'd seen of her struggle and lived through the unrelenting powerlessness of it had splintered his heart until nothing was left.

Now, he was far too fond of his own company and excessively critical of everyone else. There was Matteo to produce heirs for the Ricci legacy, and he had his work.

His brother and Angelina Bianchi were a practical match, though there did seem to be some affection between them now. Everyone knew that Angelina had had her heart set on Matteo since she was sixteen. While he'd never admit to it, he understood Matteo's initial resentment toward her.

Angelina had pointed him out to her powerful father, Vittorio Bianchi, as easily as she'd have picked a stud. Then she'd pursued him with a relentless drive that the ruthless businessman in him had to admire. When Matteo had started returning her interest in the last six months, Vittorio had sweetened the merger immediately.

Though, Alessandro hadn't agreed just because of the Bianchis' investment. Angelina had a solid head on her shoulders, was a smart businesswoman who would one day inherit the Bianchi fortune and was exactly the kind of grounding partner Matteo needed.

Hopefully Alessandro wouldn't have to deal any more with Matteo's failed business ventures, the rowdy crowd that mooched off him in return for their adulation, and the debt holes he seemed to fall into. If Angelina could get him involved in Ricci International Finances, Alessandro would have nothing to worry about.

The outline of a young woman standing outside the crowd caught his interest. Dressed in a chunky sweater, skinny jeans and dark boots, she stood out in a sea of laughing, chattering, designer-clad party guests.

The lights around the fountain cast a glow on her face, highlighting the wide, lush lips and a nose too big for her small face. Her skin was a smooth golden brown, lighter than his.

Slowly, she moved toward the wide steps leading to the villa, her long neck tilted up, the strap of her crossbody bag highlighting her slender frame and into the circle of light created by huge floodlights, exactly where she'd be best illuminated.

So that he could get his fill of her... The thought startled him. But not enough to pull his interest away.

The woman's neck moved this way and that as she surveyed the house, like a baby bird hesitant to leave its nest, fingers playing with the hem of her sweater.

Then she sighed, pulled her bag off, tugged at the hem of her sweater before peeling it off her body. A breeze pressed the silky sleeveless blouse with its high ruffled neckline against her, highlighting small breasts, a thin waist and bony hips. With her collarbones jutting out, she bordered on skinny.

A small smile played around her lips. She finger-combed her hair until it fell in waves around her face. The motion tugged her blouse upward, revealing a silky strip of her midriff. Something glinted at her belly button.

Lust was a punch to his stomach. He looked away, wondering what the hell was happening to him. Gawking at a young woman, getting hard at the mere sight of her. It was bare seconds before his gaze returned to her.

Making a pout of her lips, she applied lipstick, straightened her shoulders and started walking up the steps.

There was an innate sensuality to her movements. Something achingly real and courageous in her smile as she fought her nervousness.

He put the tumbler in his hand on the windowsill as he realized why he was drawn to her. He recognized what it took her to shake off her fears and step into the night. To step back into life. It was a step he hadn't taken in eighteen years. Not that he'd wanted to.

She possessed the same hunger for life he had known once.

Suddenly, he was sick of the cloying quietness of his bedroom, the echoing isolation of his own thoughts.

He wanted to be outside where she was, wanted to know what was so precious that she'd fought her doubts. He wanted to taste the magic of that smile on her lips, breathe it in. Steal the very real joy in it.

A fierce longing stabbed through him, reminding him that he was very much alive.

He wanted her, in whatever capacity or form he could have her.

Sam was perusing the shelves in the grand study she'd come across when she heard the heavy double doors open behind her.

When she'd finally dived into the crowd to find Matteo, it had been hard to navigate the gigantic mansion, not counting the grounds and the marquee. For all that she'd hoped that her silk blouse was an upgrade from the worn sweater, she had still stood out. Luckily, she'd wandered inside in search of Matteo and a quieter spot and happened upon this room.

Now that the moment was finally here, she felt a sudden reluctance to face Matteo. Would he appreciate her coming all the way here when he hadn't replied to her texts? Was he still mad at her for being the one to finally end their faltering relationship?

She forced herself to take a few deep breaths. The comforting scent of old books and cigars and leather instantly transported her to her grandfather's cottage she used to visit as a child. The peace and quiet of the room seeped into her skin as she walked around, centering her after the noise of the party outside.

The large mahogany desk with its worn edges, the soft leather chair with the imprint of a body, the well-thumbed pages of several books on classical music and ancient civilizations... The room was full of character. An utter contrast to the extravagant wealth outside.

It was a room that was lived in and loved well—someone's sanctuary. Just like her attic room at her parents' house. It definitely wasn't Matteo's. She rushed out of the cozy reading nook, imagining his surprise. His naughty grin. The familiar comfort of his arms around her. The way he'd always made her laugh...

The man leaning against the doors wasn't Matteo, but the one that belonged to this study.

He held a striking resemblance to Matteo, though. Where Matteo had light brown eyes, dark blond hair and features that bordered on pretty with their lushness, this man was darker, leaner, almost severe. A high forehead, deep-set eyes, sharp bridge of a nose and thin lips with a jawline that she could sharpen her mother's knives on.

Together, his features created an impression of a darkly masculine sensuousness that made her keenly aware of her own skin. Of the wild beat of her heart. Of her pulse racing madly all over her body.

If Matteo was light and charm and laughter, this man was darkness and passion and something she didn't understand. Unlike everyone else in the crowd, he didn't wear a tuxedo. Also unlike everyone else, he didn't need diamond cuff links or designer clothes to call attention to himself.

He stood with his back to the closed doors, ankles crossed, his head tilted to the side, his fathomless dark eyes taking her in greedily. As if he'd been waiting to look at her.

He was tall. So tall that at five nine, if she walked up

to him, her mouth would fit at the hollow of his throat exactly. The tight-fitting shirt hugged a leanly muscled torso and made his dull gray eyes pop. Unbuttoned to his chest, it revealed the corded column of his throat, and Sam had the insane urge to lick that hollow...

The sheer naked greed of his expression twisted her breath through her body. As if it was outside of her own control. As if he held it.

He looked at her as if he wanted to inhale her. Even having little experience with sexual chemistry, Sam knew this. As clearly as she knew the hard tug low in her belly was her response to whatever he was putting out.

She wanted to say something to break the spell, and yet she didn't want to step outside of whatever was locking them together in their own gravity. Her body felt new, full of needy claws.

Suddenly, the intensity of his stare died down. From one blink to the next. As if it were that easy for him to turn it off. Breath rushed into her lungs in a wave.

Sam blinked, feeling as if all of her insides had been splayed out for this stranger to probe. She'd had too many instances in her life where she'd felt small and powerless. But this vulnerability was different.

Embarrassment made heat crawl up her neck. "You're not Matteo," she said, a thread of complaint in her tone.

That thin-lipped mouth flinched in an imperceptible movement. He pushed off from the door, all that violent energy contained. "I'm sorry to disappoint you."

"You belong to this room, though," she added, wanting to mollify him.

"No one has ever said it like that." His gaze took in

the study, a tiny flutter of a smile at his mouth. "Point to you."

With each step he took toward her, that awareness slammed into Sam again. It was not unlike the impact she felt when she trained with a punching bag. Except she didn't know where to strike to stop it from coming at her, again and again. "You're mocking me."

He blinked. "I'm not sure I am."

Her middle felt like there was a hook there, relentlessly tugging her toward him. "Why do I have a feeling you're never unsure?"

His lips curved, slashing a dimple in one cheek. But it didn't warm the cold storminess of his eyes. "You're beautiful *and* clever."

"I'm not beautiful," she said, half to fight the effect of his words, half because they weren't true.

She was too skinny, too tall, too angular to be considered beautiful. Not that she didn't like her reflection when she saw it in the mirror. She'd survived too much at too young an age to not appreciate what she had and who she was.

Her eyes were big and wide, sure. There was a certain symmetry to her features that was pleasing, and her cousin said Sam had a body made for modeling. But she'd never been interested in modeling, and since those were ridiculously arbitrary standards society imposed on women, it didn't really make any difference to her. Life had always forced a large dose of reality on her, and she preferred it in this too. With this man, though, her protest stemmed from a place of self-preservation. "I don't like false compliments."

He stopped a couple of feet from her. Again, she had

the sense that every step he took was calculated. Raising a brow, he swept that gaze over her with such thorough possessiveness that a lick of heat trailed behind wherever it touched. When it returned to her face, challenge simmered in his eyes.

Her fingers itched to trace the slash of his brows, the sharp planes of his cheekbones. And not all of it was from the perspective of a portrait artist who was drawn to faces with character.

Frustrated at her own sharp reaction, she said, "I'm looking for Matteo."

"Did you ask the staff for him?"

"No, but he knows I'm here."

"How?"

"Are you being thick on purpose?" she asked with a familiarity she couldn't shed.

"I do not believe so," he said, his tone calm in the face of her crankiness. But there was something about his steadiness that felt hollow. As if it were simply an act. "I simply want to know how Matteo knows you're here if you didn't ask for him."

Put like that, his question was fair. "You're right. He might not know that I'm here this exact moment. But he knows that I'm here. In Italy, I mean."

"How?"

"I used the open plane ticket he gave me. The travel agent would have told him I was on my way. It's how there was a chauffeured car waiting for me at the airport."

"This plane ticket—"

"Why are you interrogating me?"

"You walked—no, *strutted*—into my house as if you were invited, Ms...?"

"Fischer," Sam said, refusing to give him her full name. Because she desperately wanted to hear it on his lips. Really, she was acting strange. "Of course I was invited. I'm not some petty thief," she said, before adding, "Now, please do me the courtesy of telling me who you are."

"Who invited you?"

"You're rude."

"I simply want to understand why you are here, Ms. Fischer."

She rubbed a finger over her temple. "Matteo invited me."

"Tonight?"

"Not specifically. He invited me months ago. It was an open invitation. I decided to surprise him. Now, tell me who you are."

"I'm Alessandro Ricci."

She recognized his name immediately. "You're the CEO of Ricci International Finances. You made that big deal recently with the software company my dad works for in California."

"Sì."

It was all starting to make sense. The extravagant wealth outside. The surname. Ricci International Finances. The resemblance between Alessandro and Matteo…

"And Matteo is…?"

"My younger half brother."

Sam pressed her hand to her neck, backing away. "So Matteo is rich, like you?"

"Sì."

Her foot caught on the rug, and the man caught her,

even though he'd been several steps away. His hand landed on her lower back. The bare patch of skin between her top and her jeans burned at the abrasive texture of his fingers. Heat from the small contact arced through her, pooling in her lower belly.

How would those fingers feel against more bare skin? Against her aching breasts? Against her belly? Against her—

Jerking away from him, she tried to corral her uneven breath.

Damn it, this man was a stranger *and* Matteo's older brother. A man so far out of her league that he might as well have been the alien overlord in one of her cousin's romance novels.

"You didn't know that Matteo comes from a wealthy family," Mr. Ricci added behind her.

"It's been years since we first met," Sam said automatically. "He did mention Lake Como but not an estate on the shores of it."

"My family owns most of the town."

She turned to face him. "Thanks for clarifying that."

His sharp gaze assessed her relentlessly. "How do you know him?"

"I've answered enough of your questions. I want to see Matteo."

"Not unless you tell me why."

"Or what?" she said, hunger and sudden exhaustion dialing up her frustration. "You'll throw me out?"

"I'm trying to save you from a potentially embarrassing situation."

Laughter burst out of Sam. "You talk just like he said

you do." Matteo had talked about his brother from time to time, but he'd never mentioned his name.

"How is that?"

"Like you know the best for everyone around you. Like arrogance and ruthlessness given shape and form. Like..."

A ghost of a smile floated on his lips. "So you know me?"

"I know of you. The perfect older brother. A cold, ruthless, brilliant man who understands machines better than people," she said, quoting Matteo word for word. She was being an awful guest, and yet something in her wanted to test his steely control.

Mr. Ricci simply watched her. And she realized what she'd thought of as a younger brother's humorous resentment held more than a grain of truth. There *was* a gloss of remoteness to him. As if he stood outside of the world and its inconvenient emotions. Like she'd been for so long.

Was that why they felt such pull toward each other?

"As much as I'd like to deny that I'm the villain Matteo painted, trust me when I say it's better for you if you tell me everything. I do know what's best for you."

"Fine. Matteo and I used to be together."

His frown turned into a full-blown scowl. "How long were you seeing each other?"

"Almost five years. I haven't seen him since we had a fight and broke up four months ago."

"Where did you two meet?"

She glared at him, but the lie came fast. "At a café in SFO."

"And he asked you out?"

"Yes, that's how these things are usually done. One interested person asks the other out," she said dryly.

Her attempt at sarcasm made no dent in his expression. "How old are you, Ms. Fischer?"

For the first time since he'd walked in, she heard cautiousness in his voice. "What does that have to do with anything?"

"Answer my question."

"Twenty-three."

Again, there was that flinch. "So you were eighteen when you two met."

"Eighteen, yes. Matteo was twenty-three," Sam protested hotly. It was the same argument she'd had with her own parents after she'd introduced them. To see her fragile little girl with a man suddenly had sent her mother into a tailspin. "I'm very mature for twenty-three," she said inanely.

Mr. Ricci snorted. Even that was elegant. "What is that you do with that mature brain of yours?"

"I'm a certified professional at annoying arrogant Italian men who treat me like a petty criminal."

He frowned, then blinked, and slowly, a beautiful smile appeared. It tugged one corner of his mouth higher than the other, digging a deep groove in the left cheek. The stark angles of his face softened, giving a glimpse into what lingered beneath the severity. If he flashed a full-blown smile at her, she might faint at the sheer beauty of it. "I'd appreciate your wit better if you answered my questions."

"I'm a portrait artist," Sam said, his reasonable tone dialing up her crankiness.

That scowl returned, and yet when he spoke, his words

were silky smooth. Too smooth, in fact. "You're the artist Matteo has been visiting every few months like clockwork for the last few years. You are Sam."

"Yep. Short for Sameera." She tried to not bristle at the distasteful note in his tone as he said her name. "I've traveled a long way to see him."

"You've wasted a long journey, especially if you were thinking of patching things up with him."

"Why?"

Those dark eyes considered her for another long moment. "Matteo is celebrating his engagement tonight. The party you almost crashed is in honor of him and his fiancée and their love."

CHAPTER TWO

Alessandro waited for tears and angry, possessive claims. Now that he knew who she was, the last thing he wanted to do was touch her again. But her golden-brown skin went alarmingly pale.

He reached her just in time. Her thigh hit his as he swung an arm around her waist loosely, giving her space to pull away. She was tall enough in her boots that her breath hit his chin. Every single point of contact of her body against his burned.

"Matteo's engaged," she whispered, then pulled away. She walked through the French doors into his private patio.

Against the glittering lake, she should have paled. Instead, the open emotions on her face made her something to behold. There was a quiet grace about her, even in her distress.

He wanted to hold her, comfort her until she was sparring with him again. He wanted to kiss that mouth until all that remained on her lips was his name. Not his brother's.

He didn't remember a time when he'd wanted someone with this naked, fierce want. All his experiences with Violetta—that first rush of love, that stage of frantic, awkward lovemaking, that fierce need to be around her all the time, to please her, to prove his worth to her had been a lifetime ago.

Forgotten, like blurry black-and-white pictures with echoes of emotions he didn't know anymore.

Dio mio, the first woman to grab his interest in years and she was Matteo's ex. Biting back a curse, he went to the stocked bar. Usually, he limited his alcohol intake to one drink per week.

In the months following Violetta's death, he'd consumed enough to damage his liver for a lifetime. Since drinking himself into an early grave would shatter his father and aunt, he'd channeled that madness into work. Tonight, however, he needed one more than one.

Because this was... *Sam. Matteo's Sam.*

The Sam that Matteo had talked about nonstop for years. The Sam that had made Matteo take unprecedented interest in overseeing their California branch. The Sam that Matteo had been very careful to not betray as a woman, letting everyone assume that Sam was just a close male friend. Why hide her existence from them?

Staring at her phone, the woman shivered.

Leather jacket and drink in hand, he went to her. Relief filled him when she let him drape the jacket over her shoulders, grabbing the edges to pull it close. "Drink this."

Her eyes flared wide. "No, thank you."

A stab of something behind his ribs made him grit his jaw. He disliked how pliable she sounded all of a sudden. "You had a shock. This will help."

"I can't. It messes with my...meds."

Shrugging, he finished the second drink. Even now,

her gaze lingered over his throat. She was mourning his brother's betrayal, and yet she watched him with such artless interest.

Alessandro wanted to taunt her for her awareness of him, but only a weak man attacked when their opponent was reeling.

"Is it Angelina Bianchi?" she said, looking out at the lake.

He studied her profile with greed he couldn't corral. "He told you about her?"

She glared at him. "That you've been pressuring him because it's a good match for the last year, yes. That you constantly push him to do more, yes. That you cast this huge shadow over his life that sometimes he can't breathe, yes."

Laughter burst out of him. Of course Matteo had painted himself as the victim. "Pace yourself, Ms. Fischer. We don't want you to exhaust yourself this early in our acquaintance, *vero*?"

"You're enjoying this, aren't you?"

"I take my words back. You're not clever at all."

She faced him, all fury and disdain. "You don't know me."

The mere hint of her temper, the fight she'd shown him earlier, creeping back into her face made Alessandro push. "Do I need to, when you blame everyone other than the man who two-timed you? And he did two-time you, Sam, because you said you broke up four months ago, but he's been seeing Angelina for at least six months already. You should be glad that your relationship already came to an end!"

"I'm not defending Matteo." Her mouth opened and closed. "I just... I don't like that you're witness to this."

Her blunt honesty took him aback for a second. "Because I refuse to sugarcoat reality?"

"Because you're too eager to pass judgment. Matteo told me that you don't date, you don't socialize. That you might as well be one of the marble busts scattered around the grounds for all the emotion you feel and—" She pressed a hand over her mouth, eyes flaring at her own daring.

"When it comes to me, Matteo told you nothing but truth."

She turned to him, big brown eyes pinning him to the spot. "I'm sorry. It's unfair to attack you. And yes, you're right that Matteo and I finished months ago. You seem to have a knack for aggravating me like no one else." She sighed. "Would a little kindness be too much?"

"Is that what you want, Ms. Fischer? A shoulder to cry on? Would it make you feel better if I took you in my arms and whispered sweet little lies that all of this was a bad dream? A small obstacle in your grand love story?"

"Oh...you *are* unbelievable."

Pushing her hands through her hair, she bundled it into a messy knot. Wavy tendrils defied her efforts, kissing her jaw.

Her breasts rose and fell, and Alessandro was perversely grateful for the color it brought back to her cheeks. He'd rather she think him an unfeeling monster than become the lost waif she'd been minutes ago. Her mouth twisted in an angry snarl as she covered the distance between them. "What I'd prefer is..." she poked him in the chest "...is for the return of my trust back to me."

"Ahhh, that I cannot do," he said clamping his fingers over her wrist. Her fingers folded into a fist, the knuckles pressing against his chest. "But if you would like to use me as a punching bag for life's disappointments, I volunteer. I'm familiar with that role, thanks to Matteo."

Her mouth dropped open, her fist resting against his chest. "That's horrible." Her outrage deflated as fast as it had come. "You're right that Matteo and I finished months ago, and in truth we should have ended long before that. But for him to move on so quickly, and to have started seeing her before we actually ended things... It's not like I can compare to a billionaire heiress."

"Self-deprecation doesn't suit you," he bit out through clenched teeth.

She side-eyed him and sighed. "For an annoying stranger I just met, you are far too right. But it's not self-deprecation. There are a lot of things I couldn't give Matteo, and I accepted it long ago."

Alessandro frowned at the ring of truth in her words. "Ms. Fischer—"

"I'd rather you don't suddenly become warm and cuddly, Mr. Ricci."

"And I'd rather you rage at me again than fall apart. I have a severe allergy to tears."

The sound that escaped her mouth was half cry, half laughter. "Was that a joke?"

Alessandro felt as if he'd achieved a personal milestone, when the doors burst open and closed with a hard thud.

Matteo's gaze swept over them, lingering on Alessandro's jacket over her shoulders.

Ms. Fischer jerked around. A reddish tint crested her

cheeks as she wrapped her arms around her midriff in a gesture he recognized as defensive.

"Sam...*cara mia*, you're here," Matteo said. "One of the staff said they saw a woman wandering around looking lost. I recognized you from the description immediately. I'm sorry I haven't been in touch. I have been busy for the last few months."

Ms. Fischer—Alessandro refused to call her Sam even in his mind—stared at Matteo. "Of course you're busy, Matteo, preparing for your engagement. Did you think I'd come up here and cause a scene if you told me? Or is it that you thought I'd never have the guts to leave my parents behind, to live my life as any normal person would?"

Alessandro frowned. It was clear she was throwing Matteo's words back at him.

Matteo raised his hands. "Give me a chance to explain."

His jacket slipped from Ms. Fischer's shoulders as she thrummed with anger. "Nothing to explain. Apparently, as much of a naïve fool that I am, I had the sense to know that our relationship had stagnated. But it was such a hit to your ego that you went and got engaged to your billionaire heiress immediately, right?"

Matteo came to her with urgent strides. Alessandro barely fought the urge to stop his brother from touching her. Instead, he bolted the door.

"How long did you play us both?" Ms. Fischer said. "You even had the gall to mention her to me, but you never had the courage to end things with me even though we both knew it had run its course."

Matteo bent his head toward her. "Sam, I—"

"Go back to your party." Ms. Fischer, it seemed, hid a spine of steel beneath the naïveté.

Alessandro rested his hip against the large desk, his fury now a slow burn. "Listen to her, Matteo."

Matteo whipped around. "Stay out of this."

"Vittorio could have been standing right next to me when you burst in here, you fool. Or any one of Angelina's thuggish cousins."

The flash of fear in Matteo's eyes said he understood the warning. "I should have checked." He cast a glance at Sam, his jaw tight. "Let's talk in private."

"You have lost your mind, as usual," Alessandro said, straightening from the desk. "Do not forget that I'm the only thing standing between you and the Bianchis if they find out about your girlfriend on the other side of the pond. Even if it is over now, they won't like the crossover. You're lucky Ms. Fischer didn't run around the party calling out your name."

"You can't understand," Matteo said with a sneer.

"*No?* You've been playing with both Angelina and Ms. Fischer. And while Ms. Fischer might forgive you, Angelina will not."

"Don't you dare lecture me—"

"I dare?" Alessandro's anger slipped its leash. "You slipped a two-million-dollar ring onto Angelina's fingers not an hour ago."

"I can't explain it. Not that you'll ever understand because you don't have a heart." His brother faced him, his mouth turned into a sneer. It had been always like this: Matteo messed up, and he cleaned up. And yet nothing but resentment festered in his brother's heart for him. "Half an hour in your company and you turned her against me."

"Stop it, Matteo," Ms. Fischer whispered, her expression stricken. "You did this. You've made me doubt our whole relationship, doubt myself."

A knock sounded, a sudden boom amidst their ridiculous standoff. "Matteo, are you in there?" came Angelina's voice.

Ms. Fischer's head jerked in Alessandro's direction, eyes wide.

She trusted *him*. Which meant he could get them all out of this predicament before Vittorio decided his family's honor had been insulted. Or that Matteo needed to be taught a lesson.

"Papà wants to give us our engagement present," called out Angelina.

Another knock came hard on the heels of her voice. "Alessandro? Is Matteo with you?" The voice of Vittorio Bianchi thundered through the hardwood. "My nephew said he saw a woman in your office. Who is it?"

Alessandro cursed. "If he even gets a whiff of you two-timing his daughter," he whispered to Matteo, "Vittorio will break your knees. I am so angry I don't think I'll stand in his way. So go along with what I say." He flicked a glance toward Ms. Fischer. "Come here, Ms. Fischer."

Matteo's glare turned sullen.

Fortunately, Ms. Fischer possessed more common sense than his brother. When she came close enough for him, Alessandro softened his tone. "Let them think you're mine. A certain familiarity will be required." He ignored the possessive satisfaction that ran through him as he made the claim. *Cristo*, he was acting worse than Matteo.

She leaned against the desk like him, leaving too much space between them. "I don't want Matteo to get into trouble." Her lush rose scent made every muscle in him curl with want. "Nor do I want to cause Ms. Bianchi distress."

Alessandro felt a fresh surge of tenderness for her soft heart. Wrapping his arm around her waist, he pulled her close. Instant heat uncurled through his middle, spreading to his limbs. Her waist was tiny, the flare of her hip where his fingers landed a sharp delineation. But there was a lean strength to her that entranced him.

Every inch of him was aware of every point of contact between them. He wanted to deepen it until she could no more think of Matteo than Alessandro could think of another woman.

She was a complication, he reminded himself. A walking, talking disaster waiting to blow up in their faces. The faster he got her out of their lives, the better for everyone involved. Including her.

And yet, he knew, with a deep conviction, that he would do everything in his power to keep her around. At least, until he could figure out what about her fascinated him so.

CHAPTER THREE

ALESSANDRO RICCI WAS the last man she should allow familiarity, Sam reminded herself.

Not that he wanted to be anywhere near her. His austere features spoke eloquently to his distaste at being thrust with her responsibility.

But the corded weight of his arm around her waist, the press of his muscled body holding her up felt like heaven. Made her want to sink into him until her exhaustion fled. Until she felt safe again.

One stolen glance at his granite jawline made her spine straighten. This man was as safe as Matteo was trustworthy.

Matteo, who had got engaged to another woman the moment they had broken up, who had been seeing Angelina Bianchi while Sam had struggled with losing interest in him. Who had probably forgotten her the moment it was over while she had called herself *weak*, *boring*, and *scared*.

She even acknowledged that her hurt came from him doing all those exciting things that she couldn't with Angelina, rather than from him falling in love with her.

Because she was a heart patient who still lived at home at the age of twenty-three, a dull woman among bold, risk-taking twentysomethings. She hadn't finished high school or gone to college or gone even on a sleepover unless it was with her cousin Kavi at her aunt's place, with her mom in the next room.

Now she was in a foreign country where she didn't know another soul. She'd hoped to repair their friendship after their breakup. The entire summer stretched in front of her, static, inert, directionless—the same as it had been for the past decade.

It had taken her so long to break away from the limitations placed on her by her body. From the rut that loneliness had placed her in. From the protective shell of her parents' suffocating love.

Without Matteo's company, where would she go? Could she look after herself? Financially, yes. Living with her parents meant she'd saved every dollar she'd earned from her summer jobs and her portrait commissions. But what would she do in Italy alone? After all the planning and months of fighting her innate fears to get herself here, should she simply turn around and go back?

Her phone pinged.

She was sure it would be a text from her mother, checking she'd arrived safely. Remembering her mother made her spiraling thoughts come to a screeching halt. If her mom discovered that Matteo was engaged, that Sam's trust in him had been misplaced—and that she herself had been right about him—she'd never let Sam live it down. Would never let her forget. She'd jump on the next plane and make an unholy spectacle until Sam had no choice but to leave with her.

Fresh anger surged through her at Matteo.

Even now, with his fiancée on the other side of the

door, he was glaring at his brother. Didn't that woman deserve better?

She despised confrontations. She'd always hated being the reason for the constant, emotionally taxing fights her parents had engaged in for so long. The guilt that they were fighting because of her, worried over her health and her future, over her long-term care, over the medical debts they'd accrued had hurt more than the pricks of the hundred needles she'd had to endure.

The thought of Matteo's fiancée, the guests at the party and his family learning about her sent a fresh tremor down her spine.

Instantly, the arm around her waist tightened, long fingers pressing into her hip without hesitation. "You'll be fine, Ms. Fischer," Mr. Ricci whispered, despite his declaration that he didn't do kindness.

Matteo flicked a dark glance at his brother's arm around her waist before he opened the doors. Ms. Bianchi was petite and curvy and vivaciously beautiful in a way that couldn't be achieved solely by designer clothes and expensive makeup. Her gaze immediately fastened on Matteo.

A large, lean man—clearly Vittorio Bianchi—surveyed them, his shrewd gaze not missing Alessandro's arm around Sam's waist. He barked something at Mr. Ricci in Italian.

Mr. Ricci shrugged in return, an arrogant smile ghosting across his lips.

Sam's cheeks burned. No doubt it was about her. And nothing decent either.

Sam breathed out a sigh as the older man left.

"Matteo, what happened?" Angelina said, tangling her arm through his.

Matteo smiled tightly. "Nothing, *cara mia*," he said, switching to English. "I wished to inquire about something with Alessandro."

"And you were shocked to find him in here with a woman?" Angelina said with a tinkling laugh. Her gaze flicked to Sam and cut away. She clearly thought Sam wasn't worth a second look.

Sam didn't know whether to feel relieved or insulted. She didn't know what to feel about anything right now. Least of all, her constant awareness of the man propping her up like a cardboard cutout.

"I know your mother wishes for Alessandro to bring a date to our wedding," Angelina said, laying her palm on Matteo's chest, "but you must trust his judgment, Matteo. If he's hiding this woman, she is not suitable company for us."

A gasp escaped Sam's mouth, a slow burn of anger humming beneath her skin.

But for her casually sexist attitude toward other women, Ms. Bianchi wasn't to blame. That Sam had to listen to it and not even offer a token protest...the fault lay with Matteo for making her face his fiancée as if she were the other woman. It also lay with Mr. Ricci, who let his friends and family talk in such a way about the women in his life.

She'd had enough. When she tried to step away, those fingers gripped the curve of her flesh tight, branding her. Tilting his head down, Mr. Ricci studied her, a mocking slant to his mouth. "Such outrage is not warranted, Ms. Fischer. Remember, you're only *pretending* to be mine."

Sam shivered as his words trickled down her spine like a lover's caress. She placed her palm on his chest, goaded beyond common sense. He was hard and hot against her fingertips. His heart thundering away belied the mockery in his eyes. "You wish I were yours. I do have standards."

His laughter enveloped her, a deep, sensual rumble, as arousing as the man's physicality. This close, she could see the warming of the gray of his eyes. The small scar across his brow. The flare of interest as he said, "And what are those?"

"No liars. And no arrogant, judgmental men who mock others' weaknesses."

The cold frost of his eyes returned. "I never mocked you."

"You aren't as inscrutable as you'd like to believe."

His gaze dipped to her mouth. It was as if one look, one word between them could generate an electric charge that surrounded them. "Or you read me better than anyone has in a long time."

"Shall we join the party, *caro*?" Angelina's loud voice cut across their murmurs.

Looking away from Mr. Ricci felt like fighting gravity.

"You shouldn't keep Vittorio waiting," Mr. Ricci said.

"You two should join us," Matteo retorted.

Sam shook her head.

A glimmer of triumph touched Mr. Ricci's mouth. "I couldn't bear to part with her right now. Go back to your party."

With a dark look at his brother, and not even a glance in her direction, Matteo left, taking his fiancée with him.

Sam jerked away from the man at her side. "I don't appreciate being fought over like a bone between two dogs."

Again those damned double doors closed. His hands tucked into pockets of his trousers, Mr. Ricci considered her. "I don't think anyone has ever called me a dog before. Not even as a boy."

"Probably because you terrified everyone around you."

"You met Angelina, got a glimpse of her father. Do you truly think I bullied you or Matteo just then?"

The openness of his question halted Sam's angry pacing. However much she wanted to blame him, this infuriatingly arrogant man was not at fault. "Fine. Don't use me as a weapon in your ongoing battle with Matteo, then. You knew that he didn't want to leave me here with you, and you still needled him."

"And it is my fault that my brother does not trust you with me?" he asked with such a straight face that Sam wanted to slap the expression off it. "Or that he risks betraying his possessiveness over an ex to Angelina's eyes?"

The discomfort Mr. Ricci caused her was of a different kind. There was something between her and this man. Something she'd never felt with Matteo or any other man.

Sam gathered her sweater, her movements clumsy. Hunger gnawed at her belly, and her head was beginning to pound too.

She threw her handbag over her shoulder and gripped it tightly to steady her fingers. By the time she turned to Mr. Ricci, sudden tears had bubbled up in her throat.

Exhaustion always made her cry. But she had to hold herself together. For some reason, it was paramount that she not show this man any weakness. She'd already betrayed her awareness of him. "If you can have my luggage located by your staff, you can be free of me."

"Now *you* are twisting my words."

"Why are you pulling your punches suddenly? Given the show you put on just now, I'm a problem for you. I need to get out of here. I need to—"

"You're not going anywhere."

"I have an extreme aversion to people telling me what I can or cannot do, Mr. Ricci."

"I don't care if you break out in hives. You look like you're ready to drop, you don't know where you are, much less where to go, and this problem isn't going to be solved by someone taking advantage of you on the streets tonight." His smooth as silk tone dissolved at the end. "Unless you're offering to leave Italy altogether. Right now."

For a split second, Sam considered saying just that. But he wouldn't believe it unless he handed her onto a flight himself. Unlike Matteo, the man was thorough. As for returning home, every inch of her rebelled at the thought.

Other than to salvage her friendship with Matteo, this whole trip had been to prove to her parents and herself that she could handle life. That meant not just physically but emotionally too, including dealing with lying ex-boyfriends and their hot-as-sin brothers.

"I can't," she said.

"Why not?"

"I can't leave without talking to Matteo, after coming this far." It wasn't a complete lie. Matteo had been such a large and constant part of her life for years. Angry as she was with him right now, that ridiculous standoff in front of an audience couldn't be their last meeting. "This vacation is important to me. Even if Matteo and I don't patch up things, I've come too far to simply turn around. I'll make other plans in a few days."

Mr. Ricci leveled a considering look at her. "He's not going to break his engagement."

Was that what he got from her admission? "You won't let him, you mean?" she retorted, just to rile him up. Of course, she'd never had any intention of getting back with Matteo.

He roughly thrust his fingers through his hair. The short haircut couldn't hide the waviness of it.

Sam smiled, wondering if it was the one rebellious element he couldn't control. Slowly, other things came into sharp focus. The grooves around his mouth hinted at tiredness as did the tight lines near his eyes.

One look at Vittorio Bianchi and the flash of fear in Matteo's eyes had told her Mr. Ricci hadn't exaggerated one bit. And while he'd been furious with Matteo, he'd made sure she didn't provoke Angelina's interest.

And yet, Matteo had treated him as if he were the enemy. She'd heard so many stories and tidbits that cast Matteo's older brother as a ruthless, uncaring tyrant who constantly belittled him.

The fairness that was a core part of her disliked that Matteo had played on her sympathetic nature, that she'd made up her mind about this man without knowing him at all. Her pinging awareness of him made everything even murkier.

"What was that smile for?" God, the man watched her like a hawk. "You looked very human just then."

He barked out a laugh, but his eyes betrayed his shock. It drew out a vicious, violent pleasure through her that she could. "Of course I'm human, Ms. Fischer. With all the flaws and desires that entails."

Her beeping watch told her it was time for her meds. While she wasn't ashamed of her condition and all that it entailed, revealing it to Mr. Ricci made her feel exposed. This need to keep a wall between them was a strong compulsion. Which was ridiculous after all the therapy she'd put into feeling normal. "I need water."

A glass of sparkling water appeared within seconds. Accepting it, she turned her body just a bit, which was stupid because he could see what she was up to if he moved an inch, and downed her meds. The bubbles tickled her throat, and her stomach made an embarrassingly loud growl.

She needed food and sleep, fast. Her body had supported her on this first journey, but she had to respect its limits. That was the most important lesson she'd learned in the last few years. "You're right. I can't just storm out of here like some hapless damsel."

His gray eyes gleamed. "I'm happy you realized the inevitability of that."

She barely fought the urge to stick her tongue out at him. "I'd appreciate it if your staff could bring me something to eat, then drive me to the nearest hotel. I promise to eat my meal quietly and leave without grabbing anyone else's attention. You can stop babysitting me."

He began shaking his head even before she'd finished. She planted her hands on her hips, exasperated. "You said you owned the whole goddamned town. Why isn't that possible?"

"I didn't say that it wasn't possible."

"Then, why are you shaking your head?"

"I would like to keep an eye on you. While you clearly possess a lot more sense than Matteo, I can't trust you to go running to him and betray your past to the Bianchis."

"I don't want to get anyone in trouble."

"But you're the one who could get him in trouble, which is why I have to control you."

Sam wanted to continue arguing with him, just for the heck of it, but she was fast losing steam. "Fine. Lock me up, for all I care, and throw away the damn key."

"Do not tempt me, Ms. Fischer."

Her head jerked up.

There was no humor in his eyes as he extended his hand. "Come."

She eyed the double doors of his study with trepidation. "I'm not a fan of big crowds and loud, noisy celebrations. With this party, I'd prefer to avoid any more speculation."

"It's a little late for that. Angelina is a huge gossip. The news of my secret liaison will have already reached my parents and all the cousins. Especially since I never bring my *entertainment* home."

As she watched, he pressed a spot behind one of the bookshelves, and an invisible door opened. A faintly illuminated, narrow corridor emerged in front of them.

Sam nearly jumped in excitement. "You have a secret corridor in your study! Do you know how many times when I was in the hos—how many times I wished to escape like this?" She looked around the high-ceilinged study with new eyes. "What *is* this place, anyway?"

His eyes crinkled at the edges. "The villa used to be

a monastery a long time ago. So there are a couple of secret passageways still intact. Not afraid of confined spaces, then?"

"Not at all."

His fingers held her elbow gently as he ushered her in. They couldn't fit side by side. Instantly, he turned to the side, fitting his body around hers. There was something so accommodating about the gesture that Sam stilled, her heart pumping overtime.

"Come, Ms. Fischer. We're both exhausted."

"That was a dirty trick you played earlier," Sam said, following him along the cool, dimly lit corridor. "You could have just said I was a friend."

"Angelina is very possessive of Matteo."

"That's not healthy," she added softly.

Mr. Ricci's grip around her arm tightened. "I'd say justifiably so, given Matteo's extracurricular activities, Ms. Fischer, *no*?"

"If you're going to make a prisoner out of me, you might as well use my name." She saw the shake of his head from behind. "Are you saying no to everything I ask on principle?"

"I have my reasons," he said cryptically. "Will you call me Alessandro, then?"

"I have a good reason to not get familiar with you."

He turned so fast that Sam stumbled into him. In the dim light, every other sense amplified. His hand on her arm, his powerful thighs pressed against hers, the thud of his heart under her fingers. The dark clove scent of him. The warmth of his exhales dancing across her lips. It felt as if she was being swallowed up by him, and the worst part was that she didn't dislike the sensation. Quite the opposite, in fact.

His gaze searched hers. "Enlighten me."

It was a miracle she hadn't the lost the thread of their conversation with so much stimulus. "I won't make the mistake of considering you a friend."

She thought that shapely mouth flinched, but at this point, she didn't trust her senses. The man would hardly care about her opinion of him. Especially when he murmured silkily, "No, you prefer men who lie to you."

"See, that's what I'm saying. Matteo messed up, bigtime. And even I did, I think. But you don't have to rub it in our faces."

He didn't move. "*You* messed up? How?"

"No way am I giving you ammunition against me."

"You don't think you're taking this enemies thing too far?" A thin thread of anger pulsed in his words. "After all, I was the one who rescued you. Did you not notice that my dear brother used the little time challenging me instead of worrying about you? It seems I am the one with your best interests at heart here."

Her exhaustion and the roller coaster of emotions she'd been through made her tongue loose. "Matteo two-timed me, yes. He broke my trust, in more than just him." She swallowed the ache. "But our relationship stagnated long ago. I clung to him instead of making a clean break like I should have long ago. Not a surprise that Matteo took the path of least resistance and went straight into Angelina's waiting arms."

She couldn't simply erase him from her life. No matter what he did, she would always consider him a friend. He'd been there for her at a time in her life when nobody else had, after all. "If there's a chance to fix our bond," she said, knowing she was playing a very dangerous game, "I'll take it. My summer is open anyway."

A flash of pure rage glowed in his eyes, burning away to nothing in a second. The faint shape of a door emerged a few feet ahead of them when he said, "My first impression of you was utterly wrong, then."

Don't ask, Sam. Don't be interested in his opinion.

All the warnings her rational mind blared were useless. "What was your first impression?" she asked in a small voice that echoed in the closed space.

"I thought you were someone who faced the truth however painful it was. Someone who dwelled in reality, instead of false dreams."

He had no idea how close he'd come to the reality of her life.

She *was* a fighter. She'd never had the luxury to live in false dreams.

But this summer was a promise she'd made to herself that she would choose living, however hard and scary that felt. That she'd choose fun and adventure and normalcy. That she'd stretch her wings and fly.

So instead of running away from a broken relationship or from a man who made her feel so much that it terrified her, instead of running back to the safety and security of her parents' love, she was staying.

She was standing on her own.

CHAPTER FOUR

CHOOSING HIS OWN bedroom to keep Ms. Fischer for the night had to be the most insane decision Alessandro had ever made.

Clearly, the stubborn waif wasn't going to change her mind about spending the summer in Milan. Which meant her past with Matteo had more chances of coming out. Which meant his ruse that she was *his mistress* was going to bite him in the ass soon.

Even the prospect of being harassed by his aunt, and the very real risk of Vittorio Bianchi's wrath, couldn't dilute the excitement that filled him at the idea of a few weeks with Ms. Fischer. He felt like a corpse that had been revived for a few days.

When he returned an hour later carrying food, it was to find Ms. Fischer sitting on the upholstered bench at the foot of his bed, clad in pajamas buttoned up all the way to her throat. An overwhelmingly protective urge rose up within him as her head lolled to the side, mouth falling open in a soft snore.

With her hair braided, she looked achingly young. Too young for him to feel that tight heat curling through his muscles.

He pushed a hand through his hair, wondering if years

of working ninety-hour weeks, of living his life within rigorously strict boundaries, had finally been broken.

He went to his haunches and gently shook her. "Ms. Fischer? Dinner is here." Cupping her shoulder, he shook her again. "Sameera...wake up." He tapped her jaw with his fingers. "Your stomach sounds like it's eating itself."

Her brown eyes flicked open, warm and soft. The most beautiful smile he'd ever seen curved her mouth. And instantly, he could imagine how she would look waking up next to him after a long night of—*Cristo*, but he was in trouble!

"Only my grandpa called me that," she whispered.

"It's a beautiful name. Did I say it right?"

Her gaze dipped to his mouth. "Better than Matteo ever has."

And just like that, with his brother's name between them, she came awake and alert. Her gaze jerked upward to meet his, the smile and its warmth disappearing instantly.

She straightened her limbs and pushed to her feet. Her brows snapped together. "You have, what...fifty rooms in this house and you bring me to your bedroom? I didn't even realize until I stepped into the shower. At least I had my bag with me, or I'd have come out smelling like...you."

A violent silence followed her irate declaration. She snapped her gaze away from him, but he saw the confused awareness. The thought of her in his shower made desire slam into him afresh. Turning away, he pointed to the lounge. "You should eat," he said, his voice hoarse.

Maybe he was losing his mind finally. It wasn't a farfetched notion. His lifestyle—his work hours, his isolation—was conducive to madness. His aunt had told him that enough times. Or maybe the part of him that he'd buried with Violetta, the part that liked companionship and affection and people even, was waking up after all these years and he had no idea how to behave anymore. Either way, he felt like he was drowning.

For once, Ms. Fischer followed his command. Slipping into his favorite armchair, she pulled the tray onto her lap.

Alessandro took the sofa opposite hers. Halfway through her dinner, she looked up. A drop of soup clung to her lower lip and she licked it away. The artlessness of the gesture only heightened his response. "Was I supposed to share with you?"

He shook his head. "You haven't touched the sandwich."

"I don't eat red meat."

"Should I have something else brought in?"

A lock of wavy hair escaped her braid and brushed her cheek. "No." She patted her belly. "The cheese, the soup, the salad and the fruit...that's actually the perfect diet for me."

"Diet?" he said, his interest snagged. "Please don't tell me you're one of those women who constantly watches what they eat, Ms. Fischer. You're skinny enough as it is."

She scrunched her nose, running a hand over her body in a self-conscious gesture. "Believe me, I know about the nonexistence of my curves." She burrowed her face into the crook of her elbow, but he heard her mutter, "Especially when you look at me next to Ms. Bianchi."

While there was a confidence about her, her comment made Alessandro wonder. "Explain about your diet."

"Oh, I meant...a Mediterranean diet is good for you. You know, lots of fruits and vegetables and seafood. But no red meat."

"For religious reasons?"

"No. I mean, my mother celebrates Hindu festivals. But she's also very much about everyone finding their own thing."

"And your father?"

"German American."

"So it's—"

"Do you interrogate everyone like this?"

"Only the ones that are a mystery."

"There's no mystery around me."

If she hadn't been shying her gaze away from his, he'd have thought nothing of it. But she did. And it made him want to know everything about her.

"I'm normal. Boring. Safe. Tame. Dull."

Alessandro frowned.

Had no one told her how her brown eyes flared when her temper rose, how her spirit shone out of her when she was challenged, how sensually she moved? "I find you anything but dull. In fact, for the first time in my life, I'm pleasantly surprised by Matteo's taste."

Her fingers stilled around the bowl of fruit. With a boldness that made his heart leap, she tilted her head and smiled up at him with an exaggerated sweetness. "That sounds awfully like a compliment."

"It is."

She fluttered the fingers on both hands in a give-it-to-me gesture. "Don't deny yourself the joy of telling me exactly what you like about me."

A pleasant warmth pooled through him. A sensation

he was beginning to associate with her. "Will you give yourself the joy of complimenting me too?"

She cupped her angular chin with her palms and studied him. Her gaze moved over his brows and his nose, landed and skidded away from his mouth. It felt so much like a physical caress that his stomach tightened. "When I find something to like about you, sure."

He threw his head back and laughed, feverish pleasure running through his veins. "*Bene.* I find you...far too interesting." If she wanted more from him, she'd have to ask for it.

She wiped her mouth with a napkin, neatly arranged everything together on the tray before she said, "So why did you bring me to your room?"

"You sound like you doubt my intentions, Ms. Fischer."

"We're back to that, then?" she said. She took a sip of water, her gaze never leaving his. "Did you bring me to your room to rattle Matteo again? Is that wise when you implied earlier that he's a loose cannon right now?"

"Is there reason for him to be rattled that you are in my bedroom?"

Was he asking her outright if she was into him? Was he hitting on her, or testing her?

It had to be the latter. Men like him didn't hit on women like her. And yet...those gray eyes held hers in a dare. The taut vein at his temple said it was no game.

What would he do if she admitted that she was attracted to him, and it was unlike anything she'd ever experienced? If she admitted that with Matteo, it had been safe and fun, whereas with Alessandro...it was a tsunami of sensations.

There was a new stringent awareness of her own body—the pulse at her neck, a tight thrum under her skin, a heaviness in her breasts that had made her cup them in the shower and an aching twinge between her legs that she couldn't get rid of no matter what she tried.

What would he do if she asked him how it felt to be so tuned in to another's breath and body, to be so unbalanced? How did one make sensible decisions in the face of this…overwhelming curiosity to explore what lay beneath?

All she'd wanted was a summer of friendly fun with Matteo. To get away from her parents, to prove to herself that she existed outside of the box she'd lived in all her life. Now she wondered if she could have this man for a summer fling and survive. Dear God, was she actually considering this?

"It's the friction in your relationship that rattles Matteo. Not anything I might or might not do."

Pushing to his feet, he gripped the nape of his neck and moved it this way and that. Had he hoped for a different answer?

He walked around, away from the window with views of the lake. Everything in the bedroom matched him, minimalistic furniture without anything softening it at all. All navies and grays, without a hint of color or warmth. The only personal touch was the grand piano taking pride of place, looking out into the lake, and the shelves and shelves of books.

"Matteo and Angelina have activities planned around the lake to celebrate their engagement. They'll be here for a few days."

Walking around, he opened the bedside drawer and

pulled out his charger. It was such a mundane thing, and yet it instantly drew her attention to the large king-size bed with navy blue sheets.

She was going to sleep in his bed, surrounded by the scent of him. Lay her head where he did every night. She'd already touched his things in the bathroom, realizing far too late that it was his. That the whole thing didn't freak her out as much as it should have.

"There's no doubt that Matteo will look for you as soon as Angelina's asleep. My bedroom is the last place he will look. Also, I'm the only one who has a key to it."

"He and I will talk at some point, you know."

Leaning one shoulder against the door, he considered her. "Of course you will. But only after the guests have left. Especially Angelina and her cousins."

"Where will you sleep?"

A wicked smile curved his lips. "It's sweet of you to worry over my comfort."

Sam rolled her eyes. "I'm worried you'll jet-set off to some exotic destination leaving me locked up here."

"I won't go anywhere until I know Matteo is not bringing Vittorio's wrath down on us."

"You'll be working at the villa for the next couple of days?"

His gaze searched her face. "What do you need?"

"Can you please arrange a car for me so that I can visit one of the art museums? That way, I'm out of here from sunup till evening. Obviously, I can't explore the beautiful grounds here without you playing my devoted keeper."

When he simply stared at her, she added, "You can come along and make sure I don't secretly contact Matteo." She couldn't stop the shiver that shook her as she looked around the dark room. "I don't like being cooped up inside."

"I'm not available to you, Ms. Fischer."

She'd expected some kind of pushback, but his bluntness made a dent in her confidence. "Assign me a bodyguard, then. I'm not staying locked up in here. Why should I be your prisoner when I can see all the art Milan has to offer?"

"There's more to it," he said stubbornly.

God, the man was infuriating. If she revealed that she hated being inside—after spending years in and out of hospitals between surgeries, in aftercare, during her parents' work hours with paid nurses—she knew he'd grant her wish. Despite his ruthless exterior, there was kindness in him. But the last thing she wanted was his pity. "How about we make a deal, Mr. Ricci?"

"What kind of a deal?"

"You get me out of here and we can discuss why you're so against Matteo and—"

"You want me to babysit you while you try to persuade me that Matteo, who's even now probably—" his jaw tightened "—with Angelina, that you and he belong together?"

Sam growled. She'd meant they could talk about his relationship with Matteo. Which was clearly more resentful than she'd imagined. Not beg him to help her patch her and Matteo's relationship. "That's not what I meant at all. You're a crude, arrogant—"

"*Buona notte*, Ms. Fischer," he said, leaving and slamming the door behind him.

Sam sat back in the chair, staring at the closed door,

his earlier words about Matteo with Angelina barely making a dent in her headspace.

Instead, Mr. Ricci occupied all of it: her awareness, her emotions, even her body's suddenly volatile need for pleasure. At his hands and mouth and that lean, powerful body.

No. She was not going there. Not with a man who'd only mock her for her attraction to him. He'd probably say she was weak or immoral for lusting over her ex's older brother.

She needed Alessandro Ricci in her life like she needed another hole in her heart.

CHAPTER FIVE

SAM SLEPT FOR thirty-six hours straight.

Vague memories drifted through her head of opening the door to Mr. Ricci in the afternoon. The poor man had needed to fetch a change of clothes.

Cheeks heating, she remembered that—in a moment of homesickness—she'd worn her oldest, most threadbare T-shirt that barely covered her panties to bed.

This morning, she'd woken up near dawn, refreshed and her body clock reset to the new time zone, to find multiple texts from Matteo. Every single one raging at Alessandro.

Frustration made her movements jerky as she packed her knapsack for the day's excursion. She was going to sneak out to an art museum in Milan. Following the list on her phone, she shoved in meds, protein bars and salted nuts, even as her mind whirled.

Why hadn't Matteo apologized for two-timing her? How dare he question her about what she and his brother were up to?

Now that she'd met Alessandro, she went over everything that Matteo had ever told her about his brother.

Matteo hadn't lied. The man was exacting, grumpy and crude but brutally honest. Ruthlessly realistic with not a hint of softness or vulnerability. But he had left out the steely core of integrity beneath.

What could dent the ironclad control of a man like that? she wondered with a feverish curiosity. What could disturb the infuriating untouchability he wore like an armor?

Sturdy sneakers in one hand, backpack in the other, she opened the door and came face-to-face with Mr. Ricci again. In a dark navy button down and black slacks, his jet-black hair slicked back, he looked austere. Even the shimmering sunlight couldn't lighten the severity of his looks.

Her breath caught afresh, that wild heat slamming into her middle as he took him in. Unlike Matteo, who spent hours in the gym and even more on his appearance, Mr. Ricci wasn't stocky or overly muscular. He was much taller than his brother and held a lean, wiry strength in his body that made her skin prickle.

A sliver of gray peeked out at one temple, but even that only added to the man's appeal.

Sam stared, fingers itching to find her sketchbook, so that she could capture his aura on paper. To somehow constrain this ruthless, powerful man to two dimensions, to contain him for herself.

A soft gasp escaped her at the sheer folly of the thought.

His gray gaze, in turn, swept over her, taking in her loose braid over her shoulder and her collarbones exposed by the wide neckline of her jumpsuit. "Dare I hope that you're leaving the country, Ms. Fischer?"

With an exaggerated sigh, she handed him her sneakers and made a show of adjusting her belt. His lips twitched as he took the sneakers, but he didn't let the smile bloom. God, the man was a miser with facial expressions.

"In your dreams, Mr. Ricci." Her fingers tingled at the slight contact with his hard chest as she reached for her shoes.

"You keep surprising me, Ms. Fischer," he said, reaching for her heavy backpack. It was such a surprising—and traditional—gesture that Sam let go without thinking.

He turned, motioning for her to follow him along a long, airy corridor. "I thought I would have to wait a few hours before I could escort you to Brera. But it looks like you've been up for a while."

Sam hurried to catch up to him so quickly that she smacked into his side and had the breath knocked out of her middle. His arm came around her waist with the firmness of a metal shackle, but even that couldn't distract her. "Did you say Brera?" she said, butterflies twirling in her belly.

He nodded, his eyes doing that sweeping thing of her face. "If I can trust you to not respond to Matteo's texts or calls just yet."

"I already agreed," Sam said, suddenly aware of the warm weight of his arm around her middle.

She stepped back and looked around. The contrasting quiet of the villa after the noise and crowd from the other night slowly sank in. As if everything else was secondary to her awareness of this man.

The corridor stretched long and cool beneath her flats, flanked by shuttered windows that spilled sunlight across inlaid marble floors. Through the open arches on one side, she caught glimpses of Lake Como glittering between cypress trees, so startlingly blue it looked unreal.

Like everything else in this house that smelled faintly of lemon oil, old money and effortless beauty.

"And?" Mr. Ricci said, without missing the slightest cue.

She sighed, hating the feeling of betraying Matteo to this...stranger. "He texted me all day yesterday. Someone also knocked on my door the previous night, but I was in a carb coma after the early dinner and wasn't fully awake."

His jaw tightened at the mention of his brother. "The evening visitor must have been my aunt."

"How do you know it wasn't Matteo?"

"He and Angelina took off for one of those lakeside crawls—bars, boat lounges, something loud, I imagine." His cool, even mildly detached, tone said exactly what he thought of such activities.

"Wait," Sam sputtered, coming to a stop just as they emerged onto the expansive front lounge. "Why would your aunt visit me?"

Mr. Ricci, of course, didn't stop.

Sam followed him down the wide stone steps of the villa, sunlight catching on the ivy-laced balustrade and the pale stucco walls that had likely witnessed centuries of extravagant splendor.

In the courtyard below, a black Mercedes waited— sleek, silent, and somehow more intimidating than flashy—and Sam tried not to gape like a tourist who'd accidentally stepped into a postcard.

"She wants to see what kind of a woman snared my interest," he said, opening the passenger door for her.

Sam inched closer, then stilled. "Why?"

"Because she hasn't seen me with any woman, in any capacity, in a long time." His eyes held hers. This close, the warm bergamot scent of him filled her nostrils. "Apparently, you're going to cause me a lot of trouble, Ms. Fischer."

Sam poked his chest and instantly regretted the action. "You're the one who declared to all and sundry that I was your...girlfriend—*mistress*, whatever your generation calls it."

Mr. Ricci grabbed her hand, his own abrasive against her smooth flesh. A jolt went through her, pooling low in her belly. His brows twitched, as if irritated by her reaction. "I offered to put you on a first-class flight back home."

"And I have already told you that this holiday is important to me." And because the man got her back up so easily, she added, "If you're worried that you'll find me moping around the dark corners of your illustrious villa, don't be. I'll find alternate accommodation soon. And I intend to have fun this holiday, with or without Matteo by my side."

He inched closer, and it was like being pulled into his gravity. "Right, I forgot how interchangeably *your* generation uses partners."

Alessandro did not have experience with being proved wrong, especially when it came to his assessment of people.

His assumption that spending three days with Ms. Fischer would rid him of his juvenile fascination with her had been rendered fully and utterly false.

In three days he'd brought Ms. Fischer to three different museums. On all three occasions, they had run into acquaintances—Angelina's cousins and even Vittorio one afternoon—and he had to play the part of a doting lover to avoid suspicion.

One morning, his aunt and father had waited on them in the courtyard, just to meet his *mysterious captive girlfriend*, as his aunt put it. It should have bothered him no end to play into the fake relationship he had created.

It didn't. If anything, he had liked touching Ms. Fischer under the pretense of an attentive lover, seeing the flush rise in her cheeks, desire dance in her eyes. Her gaze holding his in challenge even as her body quivered at their fake intimacy.

It had taken him mere minutes in the art gallery that first day to realize that she knew art, that she viewed it and absorbed it with a perspective unlike any he'd ever known. She seemed…desperately hungry for life, for any and every experience she could get.

She wasn't like any other twenty-three-year-old he'd ever met. At least not like the crowd that hung around Matteo. She was smart and witty and had no compunction about calling him out on his jaded presumptions.

He had expected a touristy American to treat Milan like a backdrop—snapping selfies in front of canvases, mispronouncing *Caravaggio*, scrolling social media endlessly.

Instead, Ms. Fischer moved through each museum like she was starving for stillness, pausing for so long in front of a single portrait it made even him restless. And when he joined her, she didn't try fill silence with inane chatter, even though the awareness between them thrummed into life. And when she spoke about brushwork or composition, it was with the clarity of someone who wasn't trying to impress him.

His need to understand why she drew him so morphed into an obsession.

How had this woman and Matteo crossed paths? They seemed to belong on different planets. She suited *his* tastes much more than those of his flashy brother and—

The thought stopped his stride, though not his gaze, as he arrived at the upscale café he'd asked the chauffeur to bring her to. Tourists and locals alike waited months for a reservation at the café, drawn by its elegant gilded ceilings that provided a perfect background for their pics.

Curled into a wrought-iron chair at the edge of the chic little spot tucked into a quiet courtyard, Ms. Fischer looked like one of the masterpieces she'd been obsessed with.

A painting in soft motion—sunlight catching the slope of her bare back as she leaned over a sketchbook. Her braid had loosened, sending flyaway tendrils to kiss the fragile line of her jaw. The low waist of her jeans dipped enough to reveal a strip of silky skin when she shifted.

The humming under his skin intensified as he watched her, as did a strange foreboding.

He hadn't been in a relationship since Violetta's death. After discovering his addictive nature when he tried to drown his pain—in drink or sex with strangers—he had effortlessly adopted celibacy as a form of control.

Cristo, he didn't remember the last time he had checked a woman out, much less wanted her with this soul-consuming intensity. And yet, here he was, pulse quickening at the sight of a woman bent over a sketchbook. A woman who was his brother's ex and far too young for him.

His fingers curled into fists at his sides—a pathetic attempt at holding on to control when he was already losing.

* * *

Sam looked up just as Alessandro's shadow stretched across the table. No wonder her pulse had been going haywire in the last few minutes.

Tall, lean, dressed in black slacks and a dove-gray shirt rolled up at the sleeves, he looked like the opposite of sun—dark but still blindingly beautiful. Power thrummed under his skin in that quiet, coiled way he had, like the threat of a storm behind glass.

Her breath caught, not because he was simply beautiful—though he was, in that severe, carved-from-marble kind of way—but because he made a long-held wish of hers come true.

It had been three days of losing herself in art. Of walking until her legs ached and her heart pounded with something other than fear, of losing herself in stories that had been told long before she'd been a speck in the scheme of life.

She felt more alive than she had in years.

"Please tell me your appetite for art has been temporarily satisfied, Ms. Fischer." His fingers moved toward her cheek and pulled back jerkily. "You look tired."

A spurt of stupid, grateful joy rose through her too fast to stop. Without thinking, she rose and wrapped her arms around him.

It was a quick hug, her cheek brushing the fabric of his shirt, arms going around his waist, his corded arm caught between her breasts. Over in the blink of an eye. Yet the scent of him—clean, sharp and expensive—coiled through her, making her limbs heavy and aching.

His body stiffened under hers even as his heart thudded violently.

Sam jerked back in a rush, embarrassed heat flooding her cheeks. She'd always been a tactile person, but she had no business touching him like that. Flustered, she moved back toward her chair too fast and almost toppled it.

"Thank you," she said, voice too bright, fiddling with the flaky cannoli on her plate.

"For what?" Alessandro asked, settling into the opposite chair.

"For calling in those favors and getting us access to those private collections," Sam said, heart still pounding. And because she hated feeling like an unsophisticated bumpkin, she added, "I guess there are some perks to being your fake, last-minute mistress. Maybe my vacation would look drastically different if I became a rich Italian's plaything for a while."

She meant it as a joke. When she looked up to meet his eyes, she realized it was anything but. The words hung between them, sharp and strange, like a spark catching in dry grass.

His gray eyes held her in a challenge. "Is that what you're looking for, now that any chance of making up with Matteo is impossible?"

Sam refused to let him provoke her. Because, for some goddamned reason, he was trying to. "Do you have no memories of being young and reckless and foolish and so achingly in love that nothing mattered?"

A sudden, raw bleakness flared in his eyes that made her stomach tighten. He looked as if he was far away, where she couldn't reach him.

Sam gripped his forearm and shook him. "Alessandro?"

Gripping his neck, he shook his head. "I do remember being in love," he said softly, shocking her anew. A fleeting flash of warmth made his gray eyes pop before they defaulted to blankness. "Feeling as if I couldn't stop smiling. As if the world was a symphony of colors and sensations. But reckless and foolish and out of touch with reality...no. I never had that luxury."

For the first time since they'd met, Sam felt the awareness between them shift and morph, fractured by something so painful that she instinctively hated it. Curiosity about his past and the fear of what she'd find battled it out inside her. "I'm sorry. I didn't mean—"

"I'm not so delicate that your paltry insults wound me, Ms. Fischer." He leaned forward over the table, pinning her under his weighty gaze. "Now I have a question for you."

She waited.

"Did you run away from home?"

Sam sighed. Of course he'd overheard her angry call with her mother yesterday. "I *am* twenty-three so the whole *running away* idea sounds wrong. But yes. How old are you?"

His nostrils flared.

Sam flushed. God, he knew what direction her thoughts were going in.

There was no mockery, no satisfaction when he said, "Thirty-eight."

Instead of serving as a deterrent, his age only made her more curious. Who was the woman he'd been talking about when he said he'd been in love? Why wasn't he with her now? Or perhaps he was in a relationship even as she had filthy dreams about him?

"Do you—" his jaw clenched "—need protection from your parents? Are they abusive?"

"What? Jeez, no." Her laughter cut off at his serious expression. "If anything, they're extra protective. Like pumped-up-on-steroids extra. They love me too much, if we can call it that. Beyond common sense and reason." His continued frown made her elaborate. "I grew up pretty sheltered. This is the first time I've ever traveled without either of them watching over me, checking my every... And I did it without telling them."

"What if Matteo had been—"

"A horrible villain who took advantage of poor old me?" she said, irritation replacing the earlier warmth. "Is there no Off button to you?"

"I'm the one who cleans up his messes."

After three days with him, Sam could see the situation objectively.

Matteo was charming, fun, larger-than-life. But she hadn't missed that he drifted into the easiest paths in life. "I've known Matteo for nearly five years," she said, wanting Alessandro to understand. "Yes, he lied to me. Yes, he started dating Angelina while we were not yet over. Yes, he got engaged to her and didn't even have the decency to tell me. But that doesn't make the entirety of our relationship a lie. I know the distinction."

"Do you? You admit your upbringing was sheltered."

Her temper flared. "Either you respect me enough to know my own mind or you don't. If it's the second, please get out."

Gray eyes gleamed with humor. "I've never been dismissed with such politeness before."

Her anger vanished as fast as it came. "I wonder anyone ever dared dismiss you at all."

He dipped his head, and a thick lock of hair flopped onto his forehead. Combined with his grin, he looked younger, much more relaxed. "So your parents do not know where you are."

God, the man had tunnel vision. "They didn't know until yesterday when I told them on the phone. They didn't know I have a valid passport and a visitor's visa. This trip was my step toward freedom."

Getting everything ready for the trip, calling the hospitals nearby, getting her travel medical insurance sorted, making sure she had enough medication for the trip, shopping for essentials, contacting friends of friends to establish a network of reliable people if the need should arise—all of it had been a big step toward trusting herself. Toward flying out of the safety of her nest. With her next step toward college all mapped out for the summer.

And she'd succeeded too.

She was here. And she hadn't fallen apart at the news of Matteo's engagement.

"Your parents were asking after Matteo on the call," Mr. Ricci prompted, deflating her imaginary fist bump.

Leaning her forearms on the table, she glared at him. "Did you listen to the entire conversation?"

"Your mother's voice was loud."

"She'll rip him to shreds if she finds out he's already engaged to someone else. The fact that she's six thousand miles away won't make any difference."

"Even without knowing that, she doesn't trust him."

"Do you miss anything?"

"When I'm interested in the subject matter? No."

The truth was that her parents had never warmed up to Matteo. Sam sighed, another knot unraveling in her mind.

Had that been Matteo's appeal—that her parents thoroughly disapproved of him? Was that why she hadn't broken up for years after she realized they weren't romantically compatible?

Her dad liked reliability and steadfastness, which made sense as he was the most dependable guy ever. Her mom thought everyone—except Sam herself, duh—should make a mark in the world with whatever abilities they had.

Matteo had possessed none of the qualities her parents wanted in a partner for their precious daughter. As if there were queues of men lining up to date someone with her history.

But Matteo had made her laugh, had made her feel like a normal girl, had given her hope. He'd been exactly what she'd needed at eighteen, having known nothing of a normal adolescence. Her friends and cousins had moved on—to colleges and new lives and new loves. She'd been too old to go back and finish high school and hadn't had enough credits to go to college, even if she could convince her mom.

She'd felt so isolated and lonely and lost.

She'd survived multiple surgeries, made it through periods of painfully slow recovery, but she'd never learned what it was to live. What to do with her time. How to connect with people.

Until Matteo had walked into the hospital café and flirted so outrageously with her that she'd spent her entire afternoon with him. He'd been the bridge that had pulled her back into her own life. He'd been her hero when she'd desperately needed one. For that alone, she'd always care for him.

She hoped that he'd cherished her friendship too, and not just as a silly diversion to build up his own ego. She needed him to understand that he'd hurt her, yes, but she could forgive him. That she still wanted him in her life.

Which made her insistent attraction to the man studying her so much worse.

"Which part did they not like?" Mr. Ricci asked, with the tenacity of a pit bull.

"Digging for dirt on Matteo is a little beneath you, don't you think?" She scoffed. "Remind me to never introduce you to my parents. Mom especially." There was no doubt in her mind that Alessandro would win them over in a second. Despite the cold remoteness, he was a natural leader, a protector.

"Why not?"

"You and she have too much in common," she said, eyeing him greedily. If she introduced him as her lover, though... Mom would blow her top. The idea sent bubbles of delight through Sam.

"You are an infuriating puzzle made of innocence and strength, Ms. Fischer." His gaze swept over as if he wanted to peel away the surface to see how she was put together. "As your parents, maybe they only see the first."

"But they should know better," she retorted, frustration coiling through her. Even as she was amazed that he saw through to what grated on her so easily. How had he gotten so close to her in three days? What dark magic did he wield? "When life hits you with hard things and you endure them, it makes you tough, ready for things you haven't experienced yet. They expect me to be brave in one thing and then try to shield me from reality in everything else. It doesn't work like that. I can't stay still so that they can feel better."

"Why are they so protective of you?"

He'd drilled down through all of that to come to the one question she didn't want to answer. His gaze stayed on her, waiting.

Sam breathed hard, wondering why she didn't want to tell him the truth. Why it mattered so much that he see her differently than everyone else in her life.

It was foolish. He'd find out sooner or later. She wasn't going to be in his life for long, and anyway she wasn't ashamed. She was a survivor.

But if she told him she'd had multiple heart surgeries by the time she turned eighteen, that she'd spent most of her teens in and out of hospitals, that she'd need medication and frequent checkups for the rest of her life, he'd look at her differently.

He'd treat her like everyone else did. As if she were fragile and needed looking after. As if her mind were also slow, not just her body. As if she were less than a normal person.

Her cousins, to this day, acted wary around her. Tiptoed around their accomplishments as if she couldn't bear to hear them. Were condescending toward her—out of love, yes, but God, it was still infuriating.

Alessandro Ricci, on the other hand, had pushed her when she'd been ready to fall apart. Had made her angry to stop her tears. He'd challenged her notions about herself until she'd no choice but to go toe-to-toe with him.

Would he still talk to her like that if he knew? Or

would he pity her too? Would he give her a different version of him—a softer, fake version?

"Ms. Fischer, come back to me."

Sam licked at her lower lip, the resolute look in his eyes telling her he wasn't going to let this go. And she was equally resolute that he see her as a woman, his equal, an object of desire.

Jesus, *an object of desire*? Why was her mind running away like this? And why was her damned body following as if an affair with this man was even within the realms of possibility?

The shrill ring of his cell phone broke the silence. He held her gaze for an eternity before he answered it.

Like a curtain being pulled shut, that austerity returned to his expression. His torrent of Italian was too rapid for her to follow.

"I have to leave. I will send another chauffeur to pick you up."

Sam nodded, his forbidding expression cutting off her questions.

Shooting to his feet, he turned, then paused. "Why do you think you messed up in your relationship too?"

Sam stared at him, even as her confusion suddenly untangled.

Matteo wanted easy, surface stuff. Forget pain, he didn't even want discomfort. He didn't want messy emotions and digging through one's feelings and assumptions and the raw awareness that could only be found beneath one's fears. The fierce realness of pleasure once you've tasted the worst kind of pain.

A life with her would never be easy or fun. And not just because she'd already tasted the primal fear of losing life itself. But because that fear had also given her an appreciation for things borne out of pain and failure and grief.

Like attraction that went beyond looks. Like the connection between her parents. Like her perception of this man's true nature within seconds of meeting him.

"I didn't understand myself and clung to him for too long," she said, finally seeing past her own insecurities. It wasn't her lack of adventurous spirit. Not her wanting to cling to the safety of her parents' home and love. Not knowing that she'd changed from the eighteen-year-old who'd found Matteo so fascinating. "I used him to feel safe, to feel good about myself."

Alessandro stared at her, unblinking, those gray eyes consuming.

Ask me what I mean, her mind chanted relentlessly.

For a man who'd pushed and prodded her from the moment she'd arrived, he backed off now. The damned man could write a thesis on how to keep her unbalanced.

"*Buona serata*, Sameera."

Sam shivered at the sound of her name on his lips. But he was already gone. "Good night, Alessandro," she whispered to herself.

It was a long time before her thoughts stilled. Before she could stop thinking of how greedy and hungry she was for another moment—quiet or sparring—with Alessandro.

For another conversation.

For another day with that dark, stormy gaze consuming her.

CHAPTER SIX

AFTER BEING ALONE at the villa for two days, Sam began to feel like a hapless heroine in a gothic novel, creeping along its marble-tiled hallways. She hadn't seen either Alessandro or Matteo since the chauffeur had brought her back from the café. Their parents and Angelina and her thuggish cousins, everyone had been gone.

The villa, so breathtaking and boisterous when she'd arrived, now felt cavernous and quiet. As if to add to the dreary ambience, the rain hadn't let up once. Just sheet after endless sheet of gray falling over the lake, blurring the view into something shapeless and cold.

She'd tried asking the staff where Mr. Ricci and the rest of the family were, but they just smiled politely, while bringing her endless meals. In the end, she'd taken to curling up in the armchair in Alessandro's study and sketching him from memory, as if that might conjure him out of thin air.

Worried that the Bianchis might've gotten wind of her or that Matteo was in trouble, she stayed put.

Alessandro didn't owe her anything, of course. Not as his fake mistress. Not as his reckless little brother's ex. Not as an unwanted guest. But two days of radio silence while being stuck at a palatial mansion would make *anyone* cranky.

Watching hour upon hour pass was as painful as waiting for her number to come up for surgery years ago.

What she loathed the most was the needling thought that Alessandro, back in his sophisticated life, had forgotten the naïve, dull, boring Ms. Fischer.

The last of the sun's rays were dancing over the lake when the bedroom door opened to reveal Alessandro.

Dark shadows clung to his eyes as he stilled and stared at her. His gray shirt was rumpled, and his wavy hair was in such disarray that it was clear he'd tugged at it.

Legs trembling, Sam came to her feet just as he said, "Is something wrong, Ms. Fischer? You look troubled."

Usually, she wasn't an overly emotional person. It had been drilled into her that stress could kill her, literally. But this man was like a specially designed aggravation machine. "No, I'm not okay. You left me here, and your staff wouldn't say anything." She fisted her hands. "I expect that from Matteo, not you."

The flare of his nostrils told Sam what she'd just blurted out.

"I apologize. I didn't have your—"

"You must have told yourself the poor fool has neither the choice nor the self-respect to walk away," Sam said, cutting him off.

He reached for her, and she jerked away. "I thought no such thing."

Tears clogged up her throat. "Nothing justifies leaving me here like some rotting vegetable in the fridge. You made fun of me from the moment I showed up—"

"Matteo had an accident."

"What? When? How is he?"

"He was driving his motorbike and took a curve too fast. He has multiple fractures in his legs, and he hit his head. They worried he'd slip into a coma, but he gained consciousness two hours ago." His exhaustion weighed down the words. "I left the hospital for the first time since they called me at the café."

"Wait, that was the phone call you got? Why didn't you tell me?"

"Sameera, look at me."

She lifted wary eyes to his face. Exhaustion was etched into his sharp features, making him look even more austere than usual. "I couldn't think straight. All they said on the phone was that he had an accident. When I arrived, though..." A groan rattled through him. "I would not have left you alone for so long out of choice. Say you believe me."

She nodded, even though his request was a demand. As if it was imperative that her trust in him wasn't broken. "I thought I got Matteo into trouble with the Bianchis and that you hated me—"

"Shh, *tesoro*. Take a deep breath." His arm came around her waist, and she fell into his embrace, like a puppy starved for attention. He pressed his mouth at her temple, his breath warm on her skin.

Sam thumped at his chest, as if he were her very own punching bag. "Stop ordering me around. I'll push myself into hysterics, if that's what I want."

He fell back against the wall, taking her with him. Her body jostled against his, sending a different kind of shiver down her spine. "You have every right to be angry," he whispered, dry humor coloring his tone. "But I didn't forget about you for a minute. I left the hospital the instant I was free. I needed to explain in person."

Her anger over him had had two whole days to build, but it blew out of her in two seconds flat. "Is he still in danger?"

"He's slipping in and out of consciousness, but there's no risk of him falling into a coma."

She buried her face in his chest, worry twisting her stomach. "Whatever Matteo's faults, he's my friend. My anchor to the world when I…" She swallowed the lump of tears in her throat.

The corded arm around her loosened. Alessandro's hand lifted and hovered over her face, an uncharacteristic hesitation in his eyes. "I'm sorry I made you defensive about your relationship."

Standing so close, Sam felt the tension in his lean body. How his movements were taut and economic when he touched her, as if he didn't want to cross his predetermined limit.

She pushed back and instantly missed the warmth of his body. "How are *you* doing?"

A ghost of a smile tipped up the corner of his mouth. "I'm fine now."

"Will Matteo get back to normal?" That she was asking the question to probe into his heart as much as for info on Matteo was not lost on her. When he gave her that condescending expression she was beginning to know well, she held up a hand. "Not the version you told your parents or Angelina."

"Everyone wants optimism and faith from me. Not you?"

Now that she could see beyond her own distress, now

that she was beginning to know the man beneath the remoteness, she saw the strain of the past few days in his eyes, the worry lines digging deep grooves around his mouth. If the truth was painful, she wanted to give him the small comfort of not bearing it alone. "No one should have to shoulder life alone."

His gaze clung to hers. "I'm used to it."

"But I'm here now."

His chin dipping, he looked taken aback. As if she had morphed into someone else right in front of his eyes.

"I've handled hard things in life, Alessandro."

"I'm beginning to see that." He walked past her into the room and opened a bottle of sparkling water. When he raised one in her direction, Sam shook her head.

She watched the play of the muscles at his throat. His tone was flat when he spoke. "Matteo will need at least two more surgeries. Many months of physical therapy to build back strength in his right leg. But yes, he can make a complete recovery."

Sam threw herself at him, joy overriding any sensible caution. "Thank God!"

He caught her, and this time his arms went around her. From chest to abdomen, she was plastered against his powerful body. All that ache in her breasts came back with a twofold intensity. This time, their embrace didn't soothe her. It sparked that hunger that never seemed to be far. He was deliciously hard and lean against her, and all Sam wanted was to press her hips closer, lean her thighs against his until she could feel every inch of him intimately. Until she could provoke his hunger too.

Gentle but firm hands nudged her back. "From enemies to such a warm embrace," he said, clearing his throat, "that's quite a turnaround."

"I never said we were enemies. I admit you're growing on me."

One brow arched in that arrogant face. But that conscious movement couldn't hide the flash of desire in his eyes. For the first time in her life, Sam bemoaned her lack of sophistication when it came to sex and attraction and affairs.

Walking around the lounge, she picked up the loose sketching paper, books and other stuff she'd scattered about. The bedroom was as much hers now as it was his. "Matteo's been through hard stuff before, right? He told me his asthma had been really bad. That he was teased at school mercilessly for being a small, scrawny kid and you stopped some bully who made his life hell."

"He confided in you?"

"He said he was a runt next to you. But that he overcame..." She sighed. "You're surprised he told me."

"Matteo likes to pretend that he was never weak. He sulks when my aunt reminds him of the almost fatal episode he had once. I think he's even convinced himself that he was always this charming and dynamic."

Sam hugged her sketch pad to her chest. "Is it such a bad thing if you don't want everyone to know your weaknesses?"

"If they make you ashamed, yes," he said, casually picking up her hairclip and her two pencils, before settling into the armchair that had the perfect view of the lake.

Awareness zipped down her spine at how easily this ruthless, powerful man seemed to have accepted her presence—and her innumerable things—in his room. As if she belonged there with him.

"Matteo is ashamed of his physical vulnerabilities and goes to any lengths to make up for them."

She stared, arrested, at the picture he made.

Head thrown back against the chair, long legs sprawled in front of him, with her pink hairclip clasped between elegant fingers, Alessandro was all subdued vitality and masculine perfection. Even with his hair and shirt rumpled, he looked like he belonged on the cover of a magazine.

And she could see how being compared to this man—who was a natural leader—would've bred resentment in Matteo. Being ruthlessly perfect himself, Alessandro would demand the best of everyone. "Does he know that you don't think he has anything to be ashamed of?"

"Does he think I'm a complete monster?" He bit out what sounded like a curse, as if he'd found the answer to his own question. "If anything can defeat Matteo's recovery, it will be himself. Hard work and endurance are not his strong suits."

"He has us to help him with that," she said eagerly. She knew what it felt to not have control of one's body.

His gray eyes flicked open and pinned her to the spot. "Does he have you, Ms. Fischer?" His feet kicked off the ottoman before he added, "To cheer him on?"

Sam could feel her cheeks heating. He had phrased it like that on purpose. She walked around the lounge to the seat opposite him, taking her time before saying, "Yes."

"A prolonged stay will complicate things."

It wasn't quite a warning, and yet there was something in his tone. "Life is full of those pesky complications."

"You will continue to pose as my girlfriend so as not to arouse any suspicion with the Bianchis."

"That sounds like a promotion from mistress. At least in title," she said brazening it out. "Does that mean you can tolerate me now?"

The infuriating man just watched her from under those lashes. "Once my aunt gets her hands on you, you might change your mind. Especially when she realizes you will be the thing that helps her manage her worry about Matteo."

"If I can distract her, I can bear that much."

Leaning forward, his gaze did that thorough sweep of her again, as if he wanted to unravel her and see how she was put together. "I'm beginning to think there's more to my brother than I give him credit for. He gained such loyalty from two intelligent, beautiful women."

"I can absolutely see why he would pit himself against you and come up wanting," she said before she realized it.

Heat poured through her. But she didn't want to take it back.

She wanted to be this girl—no, this woman—who saw a powerful, ruthless man like Alessandro for what he was underneath his remote, aloof armor.

This woman who didn't hide from her own wants.

This woman who boldly challenged a man who would devour her given half the chance. But what if she wanted to be devoured?

What if after everything she'd been through, she'd morphed into a dark, hungry creature who liked grumpy monsters better than charming next-door guys?

Her heart pounded in her chest, her skin felt deliciously taut, and there was that fluttering ache between her thighs… For the first time in her life, she was standing in the arena, instead of watching from the crowd.

Alessandro didn't move a muscle, like a wildcat lounging in its true habitat but tracking every breath and move of its prey. Every inch of him was focused on her. "Because I'm taller, richer and more handsome, *bella*?"

The endearment landed right below her belly like a fishhook, pulling at her entire being. "Matteo is definitely the more handsome one," she said, folding her arms under her breasts, which felt achy and heavy.

"What, then?" The intensity of his gaze made her skin prickle, as if she were standing too close to a flame.

"He knows that, beneath the arrogance and the remoteness, you've got him beat. That you're real, Alessandro. For someone like Matteo, who dwells in illusions, he tells the world and himself you'll always be a threat."

"You're a very dangerous woman, Sameera."

She shrugged, her breath coming in a ragged push. Luckily, she was saved from having to reply by his cell phone.

Her pulse raced as she watched him answer the call, his gaze on her the entire time. He hung up within a few minutes, pocketed his phone and went back to his lounging. With his eyes closed, the dark circles under his eyes looked like bruises.

"When was the last time you went to bed?"

"Are you worried about me?"

"Does *anyone* worry about you?"

"They don't have to."

"That's a very lonely place to be."

His lashes lifted. "You continue to amaze me, *bella*."

"Don't mock my concern. It's genuine."

He dipped his head. "I haven't gone near a bed in three days, no. I did eat, at the hospital café. I had to finalize merger documents for a Japanese company. I grabbed a quick shower at work. Then I went back to the hospital to talk to the specialist. My father is a steady man but my aunt…is falling apart." A soft sigh escaped his lips. It was only when he mentioned his aunt that Sam heard the catch in his voice. "Somehow, I managed to talk her into coming home tonight so that she can rest. Right now, Angelina is with him. As soon as I can muster some energy, I will go back to the hospital and stay with him tonight. The second surgery is scheduled for first thing tomorrow."

"I wish I could stay with him for the night. But hospitals…" she said. "I've had some bad experiences."

"You don't have to."

Sam pushed to her feet, feeling as strung out as she'd felt after the flight. But this exhaustion was less physical and more emotional. Like she'd lived through a year's worth of experiences in a week. "Can I see him tomorrow?"

"Sì."

"You should nap," she said, gathering her painting supplies. "I'll go for a walk."

He flicked a hand in her direction. *"No,* stay."

"You need a break."

"I like your company."

She went a few more steps.

"Per favore, Sameera."

She turned around to find that perceptive gaze watching her. "Why do you do that?"

"Say *please*?"

"Call me Sameera in such a..." She blew out a breath. "Why can't you just call me Sam?"

A casual shrug which didn't fool her at all.

"Tell me, Alessandro. Now."

"I like you best like this, *bella*."

The man disarmed her like no one could. "Like how?"

"All fierce and demanding."

Sam swallowed. He lit a fire in her body with a simple sentence, and took up space and familiarity with her as if it were his birthright. From the first moment, he'd given her honesty, realness and himself. "Answer my question."

His chin lifted from his chest. "Sam is his name for you."

Shock made her stare at him for long minutes. There had been distaste but also something so...*possessive, so feral* in that answer. Her breath shallowed. "What?"

"When I hear *Sam*," he continued softly, "I hear it in Matteo's voice. All those years gushing about you. *Sam's great. Sam's wonderful. There's no one like Sam.* I didn't realize you were a woman. But now I know. You are *his* Sam."

You are his Sam.

His words echoed through her, raising a hundred questions.

Reaching him, she extended her hand and slightly pushed down on one hard shoulder. The tension in his frame pinged between them, taut and throbbing. Cupping his face, she tilted his jaw just so, and then she reached up to push the lock of hair that fell on his forehead.

His long fingers wrapped around her wrist and held. With one slight shift, he buried his jaw in her palm. His heavy breath made his body shudder. And with her other hand resting on his shoulder, Sam felt every bit of it. Felt the hunger and heat rise in him and envelop her.

Heart pounding, her fingers fluttered, tingling to touch more of him, to trace every angle and plane of his face. His mouth, open and warm, rested against the base of her palm, his breath coasting against the underside of her wrist. Her chest rose and fell, and every muscle in her shivered.

All she wanted was to keep her hand there and sink into his lap. Tug his head down so that she could kiss that mouth. Tell him that she hadn't been Matteo's Sam for a while. Taunt him until he couldn't switch it off anymore. Tempt him until he eased the constant ache she felt at her core.

In the blink of an eye, he let her go, until she was standing by him, her hands dangling by her sides.

"Sameera?"

She jerked away and reached for a glass of water just to give herself something to do. "Hmm?"

"Before Matteo woke up, when the risk of coma was high...it struck me—the source of poison in our relationship—where it had begun. I won't bore you with how it started. Both of us have let the resentment fester. When I saw him at the hospital, I hated that I never even wished to fix it. Never tried to understand things from his perspective." Sam could feel his gaze on her face, but she stubbornly kept hers turned away. "But I love him. If he hadn't recovered—"

"But he did," she said, loudly. "Soon, Matteo will be back to his vital, wonderful self."

"*Sì*, he will. Even if I have to make him take each

step." His Adam's apple moved. "See, you and I do have something in common."

"What?" Sam asked, even though she knew what was coming. It was like waiting for the punching bag to hit you back but not knowing when it might happen.

"We both want him to get better. We both love him, *sì*? You will agree then that we can't do anything that would hurt him."

Sam looked at him then, her breath hitching.

It took her an eternity to fix her erratic breathing, to shove away the splintering hurt within her to one corner and lock it up.

When she sat down and began sketching quietly, his eyes closed. For all his brutally honest ways, he'd rejected her in a roundabout way. Stopped her before she made a fool of herself.

Maybe she'd been fooling herself that the pull between them was strong on his side too. Maybe he wasn't into women who threw themselves at him.

Maybe he saw her as an interesting anomaly in Matteo's life and nothing else.

No, he wanted her.

She knew that as well as the unshed tears crowding her eyes as she captured the beautiful lines of his face.

Alessandro stayed still and quiet for how long he had no idea. At least the violent tremors that had taken hold of him earlier had subsided. But he couldn't relax.

Rejecting her, killing the tug of open desire in her eyes, had been the hardest thing he'd ever done. Pushing away from her touch—that he still felt on his jaw like some sort of phantom caress—was like kicking himself when he was already down.

Because after two days of trying to make sense of his world crashing down on him, of coming to terms with his grief and guilt and powerlessness as Matteo lay pale and unconscious in the hospital bed, all he wanted was to lose himself in the compassion in her eyes, in the strength she offered with her words, in the inviting warmth of her body.

She made him forget effortlessly—her fists as they landed on his chest, her body clinging to his offering solace and escape, her words, probing and seeking and giving—everything about her felt like salvation. A relief from the agony of wondering if he'd lose his brother before he could fix their relationship.

But he'd forced himself to remember who she was. He'd rejected her, knowing that he was hurting her. It hurt him a thousandfold to see her retreat. To see the sheen of tears in her eyes. To see her struggle to pull up her armor.

Now the only sounds in the room were the scratch of her pencil against paper and the thundering roar of his own heart in his ears.

Her gaze touched every inch of his face, lingered on his mouth. Even aware that all she saw was a subject, his body still reacted. He was exhausted to the bone, his control in shreds. All he wanted to do was to hold her again, bury his face in her warm neck, pick her up in his arms and take her to bed.

And stay there, for as long as it took to convince her that he wanted her. That he was shaking with need to kiss that soft mouth. That he wanted to make her smile again, wanted her to spar with him again. That he wanted that hand of hers to drift all over him, as she'd been thinking earlier.

Even while he'd been waiting for Matteo to wake up, he hadn't stopped thinking about her. How would she take the news? Would she fall apart? Or would she realize the depth of her feelings for him and want him back?

Selfish as he was, the last scenario had gnawed away at him. The prospect of seeing them back together made him want to throw up. His relief that, while she loved Matteo, she didn't want to be back with him made him shake like a leaf.

There was an inexplicable fragility about her that was a reminder that he did not know all of her. Violetta, before she'd fallen sick, had been bold, vivacious, a lioness of a woman.

But Sameera's strength was more subtle, more nuanced.

It lay in her heart.

Her bold claim that no one should shoulder life alone, that she would hold his hand through this was as painfully real and arousing as her lean, lithe body pressed up against him.

For the first time in more than a decade, Alessandro wanted something with a soul-deep need.

But the same intense desire that was tying him up in knots, that had him shaking like a teenage boy at the mercy of his libido, was also a blaring warning sign.

She unraveled him with her honest words and her genuine concern and her tentative touches. Her fingers on his hand felt more arousing than another woman's mouth on his cock. He swallowed at the filthy images that thought brought on, with her in all of them now. His erection pushed against his trousers. If her gaze dipped below his chest, she'd see it clearly outlined. But it didn't move past his chin.

In the hour that they sat in silence, she didn't look at him again as anything other than a subject, her will as steely as her smile could be soft.

In that first moment of consciousness, Matteo had asked for Sam. Not his mother who hadn't left his side. Not Angelina whose vivacity had gone out. Not their father or Alessandro.

'Sam... I want to see her. I want to tell her that I...' The rest had been lost as he'd slipped back to sleep.

The last thing Alessandro could do while his brother was unconscious in a sterile hospital bed was kiss his girl or his ex or whatever the hell Sameera was to him.

He opened his eyes to find Sameera looking at him but not really seeing him. He, on the other hand, watched her with shameless abandon, lust stabbing through him like an incessant bell.

Her wide lips were wrapped around a pencil while her hair lovingly framed her face. The worn-out crop top showed her navel. He wanted to peel that top off and kiss her all over. He wanted to tongue her belly button and tug at that diamond stud with his teeth. He wanted to dip his fingers into those tight leggings she wore and discover if she was wet for him.

He wanted to make her come on his fingers, mark her skin with light bruises. He wanted to make her smile and laugh, cry and scream, writhe and moan beneath him. He wanted to bury himself so deep inside her that he was a part of the aching loveliness of her spirit and body.

Cristo, he wanted her.

In that moment where his imagination lured him into filthy places, he admitted the truth to himself. Matteo was nothing but an excuse he was using to stop himself.

Because Sameera was not meant for men like him.

If he touched her, he could show her everything she wanted to taste, but after…he would discard her. He was empty to give her what she needed.

If he knew one thing about the woman who made him realize how empty his life was, it was that she wasn't made to be used and discarded, even if she were a willing participant.

Sam was made for forevers made up of long, cold nights and bright sun-kissed days, filled with laughter and love and joy and connection.

And he'd already had his forever—a flicker flame of joy followed by lifelong kiss of pain.

CHAPTER SEVEN

It was another week before Matteo was brought home and settled comfortably with round-the-clock nurses.

Sam visited him once at the hospital when Angelina had been elsewhere, and he'd been unconscious the whole time. That trip into Milan in a chauffeured car with Alessandro had been unbearable. His extreme solicitousness, as if she were a stranger, had made her want to scratch her nails down his face.

Back home now, Matteo on painkillers mostly slept.

Sam was desperate to tell him she'd forgiven him, that she didn't want to lose him. She wanted to share her confusion about his brother with him, as inappropriate as that sounded. And she wanted to hug him and see him laugh.

More than anything, she didn't want to stay another minute at the villa. Not in Alessandro's bedroom, not in his bed.

Because even when he avoided her, he was entrenching himself into her very thoughts. The morning after she'd begun sketching him, she'd been shown to an airy, sunny room on the second floor where a variety of painting supplies had been waiting for her in pristine, unopened packages. Complete with two new smocks.

Another shock had been when her mom had called two days later, doing a complete one-eighty, asking Sam to live it up and have fun.

Because the great and mighty Alessandro Ricci of Ricci International Finances had personally called to reassure her parents that she was being looked after very thoroughly. In a few minutes of transatlantic conversation, Alessandro had achieved what Sam hadn't been able to achieve her entire life: talked her mom down from the ledge.

He didn't step into her bedroom—*his bedroom*—anymore. There were no more needling remarks to make her gasp, no probing to make her react, no penetrating looks that made her want to burrow into him. Just unrelenting politeness.

He'd put distance between them, distance the blasted man should've kept when he'd found her waiting in his study for his brother. Instead, he'd let her see him, know him. Made her want him.

Yep, she was blaming it all on him.

Unbearable as it was to be subjected to his politeness, on top of Alessandro's aunt's interest in her, Sam couldn't bring up leaving. At least until she was finally able to talk to Matteo.

One bright morning a week after Matteo's arrival home, his parents were arguing in the kitchen in a volley of Italian that enveloped Sam.

Outside the French doors, sunlight shimmered on the lake, and inside the kitchen the scent of coffee and croissants pervaded.

Antonio Ricci—an older, warmer and more smiling

version of Alessandro—whispered something to his wife Maria that made the older woman smile softly.

Alessandro's aunt was a lovely woman, but Sam was glad she spoke little English. Maria asked a lot of questions about her and Alessandro. *Girlfriend, affair, marriage* and *babies* were words she said so frequently in Italian that Sam had been compelled to learn their English translations.

A surge of homesickness hit her as she watched the clear affection between the older couple. Never far behind, as always, was guilt. She had clear memories of her parents like this, arguing with smiles, kissing each other in the kitchen, competing about whose side of her heritage Sam would learn more about. And then, on a beautiful day like this, she'd collapsed and they'd begun falling apart.

God, she wanted them to be happy so badly that her stomach knotted every time she thought of them.

"Sameera, *stai bene, cara mia?*"

Coloring, Sam smiled at Maria. "I'm fine, thank you. Just lost in thought."

"You miss Alessandro, *sì?*"

Sam nodded, because it was easier to go along with Mrs. Ricci than explain the twisted complexity of her nonrelationship with Alessandro, who'd been on a trip the last two days.

At least she hadn't been forced to socialize with Angelina who'd been ordered by Alessandro to limit her visits to the villa to see Matteo to mornings. Especially since she came with an entourage of cousins and bodyguards.

If Sam didn't know Alessandro as well as she did, she'd have thought it a lucky coincidence. But he knew she painted in the morning and took an online class in the afternoon and that it kept her out of Angelina's way.

She was glad to sit with Matteo after dinner when Maria's energy lagged. That Maria didn't wonder that Sam spent more time with a sleeping Matteo than an awake Alessandro was just pure luck.

She'd just poured herself a cup of freshly squeezed orange juice when Angelina, thankfully alone for once, entered the kitchen. Sam froze, taking in the simple beige shirt and dark trousers that did nothing to dampen the woman's beauty. She turned toward the doors when Angelina blocked her, her temper in full control of her.

Before Sam could blink, Angelina grabbed the cup from her and threw it in Sam's face.

Sam gasped at the cold slosh of the liquid on her skin preceding the jarring thump of the glass against her shoulder. The sound of it breaking against the marble floor made her falter.

Pain shot through her bare foot as a piece pierced the skin.

A torrent of Italian filled the room as she was bodily lifted from behind. She knew that scent, that body, even the warmth reaching for her. Relief surged through her as she sank into Alessandro.

"*Porca miseria!* Did she hurt you?" Gentle fingers dabbed at her face. "Look at me, *tesoro*."

"It was just orange juice," Sam said trying to corral her shuddering relief. "I'm fine, Alessandro. She scared me. But it was more…"

He lifted her onto the breakfast table, cutting her words off. "There's a shard stuck on top of your foot"

"Yes and…"

"*Zia*, bring me the first-aid box." He turned around, his back a tense wall. "How dare you treat my guest like that?" His words were soft, slow and yet the quiet rage in them fell like a shroud on the room.

"Matteo is dying because of her." Angelina's voice quivered. "While she—"

"*Dio mio*, Matteo is not dying. Sam is not the reason—"

"She is. She made him crash the bike. He was not happy since she came. You have to throw her out—"

"She isn't leaving," Alessandro bit out in that quiet voice that would've been less scary if he'd shouted.

"Then I will ask my father—"

"*Sam. Is. Mine.*" Each word dropped like a crashing cymbal into the space. "If you touch her again, if you so much as come near her, I'll cut you out of Matteo's life. Permanently." Sam gasped at the vehemence in his tone. "I do not give a damn if your father rules all of Milan. You crossed a line."

"Alessandro, wait—" Sam started before he cut her off.

"You're not welcome in my house anymore. Get out."

Brown eyes filled with shock, Angelina stared at him.

"Alessandro, you can't simply throw her out," Sam said, her words drowned out by his aunt begging the same.

"Stay out of this, Sameera."

Italian flew back and forth between him, his parents and Angelina, but he didn't relent. The quiet rage in his eyes when he checked her face made her swallow.

He felt guilty for not protecting her, she knew. Guilt and pity and politeness weren't what she wanted from him. Still, pathetic as she was, she couldn't help touching him. She bent her forehead to his back, clutching the taut muscles of his biceps. "Alessandro, give her a chance to explain."

"There is nothing to explain," his voice softened instantly, the muscles clenching under her touch. "Papà, get her out of the house. If she makes a fuss, call security."

A thundering silence followed his harsh dictate.

Antonio sent Sam a reassuring glance before he walked a hysterical Angelina out. Still, she cast an astonished look at Alessandro's protective stance around Sam.

The moment she left, Alessandro pushed in to stand between her legs.

Her belly rolled, sensation making her thighs quiver. When she looked up, his face was a taut mask. The man wasn't even aware how provocative their positions looked.

Sam flushed as his aunt approached, a first-aid kit in her hand.

"Leave us, *Zia*."

Maria gave Sam a quizzical look and left.

Deafening tension crackled around them. Sounds from the outside breezed into the room, the table dappled in bright morning light as if the universe itself was orchestrating the moment. That sharp pain persisted in her foot, but the feel of Alessandro's powerful thighs pushing hers wide apart trumped every other sensation. Awareness pulsed with a vengeance between her thighs.

With that tightness to his movements that betrayed his lack of control, he undid the cuffs of his dress shirt and pushed the sleeves back. The sight of his corded forearms sprinkled with dark hair made her think of those arms holding her down, of those long fingers touching her everywhere.

God, everything about the man made her think of sex.

"Alessandro…" she said, suddenly glad for Angelina's stunt. Which made her more than a little twisted in the head. "It was just juice—"

Pushing the wooden bench back, he brought her foot to his thigh. Even the sight of her foot in his large, elegant hands made her core flutter. Not looking at her, he laid out a bunch of things from the kit on the dark wood of the table.

Sam pressed her heel into the hard muscle while he, with infinite care, pulled out the shard stuck in her foot. Her heart expanded to dangerous proportions as she watched him clean up the cut, apply an antibiotic and wrap her foot in layers of gauze.

A muscle jumped in his cheek as he packed up the supplies. "Do you still think I'm overreacting?"

"I never thought that." Gripping his wrist, she whispered, "Won't you look at me?"

Those long lashes lifted, and the cocktail of emotions there made her swallow.

Not because she was afraid of him. Never.

But she'd never seen him at the edge of control like this. The devil in her wanted to push a little more to see what she could get out of it. God, when had she become so conniving? "You're very angry."

"What if it had been hot soup or that ginger chai you drink in the mornings?"

How was she not supposed to feel flattered by the fact that he didn't miss a single thing about her? "It wasn't."

"She could have seriously hurt you."

"She scared me, yes, but she didn't hurt me. What she wanted more than anything was to make herself feel better."

Eyes wide, he looked at her as if she'd lost her mind. Sam was thinking the same. But for other reasons. "How would you know this?"

"I have a cousin like her, a total diva. And I've seen the lingering panic in Angelina's eyes. She's scared that she'll lose Matteo. To something worse than me. I'm the option she can control. If you'd given me a moment with her, I could—"

His scowl deepened. "You're not going near her."

"And who are you to order me around?"

"*Per piacere*, Sam. Do not push me around right now."

"You called me Sam," she whispered, beaming wide. Her foot hurt, her heart was getting entangled in this man, but that he called her Sam was enough to send her on a fizzy trip.

He looked at her, finally. Properly looked into her eyes. And the hook was back in her lower belly tugging and pulling her into those gray depths.

"I don't want to fight with you about her," she said in a low whisper.

A soft, breathtaking smile lifted the edge of his mouth. It was like standing in a patch of sunshine created just for her. "And here I thought you loved nothing more than to put me in my place."

Lifting her hand, Sam almost touched the groove the smile dug in one cheek. "I miss you," she said, her fingers hovering over his jaw.

Every inch of her wanted to touch him, to mark him. To claim every small part of him as her own. Beginning with that smile. If it were up to her, she'd make sure everyone knew they belonged to her. The ones where his gray eyes turned warm and one corner of his mouth tugged up...they came out for her, only her.

He tensed. "You *miss* me?" he said slowly, as if he couldn't quite get the texture of the words on his lips.

Embarrassment flooded her. But she couldn't do coy or smooth or flirty. She'd missed all the stages where she'd have liked simple, easy boys. Instead, life had made her skip them all and brought her here to this man.

This remote, ruthless, yet inherently kind man who was determined to keep her at arm's length. Whose gray eyes betrayed his longing. Who said so much with his actions and nothing with his words.

"I do, yes." She clasped her hands back in her lap. "Between Mom and your aunt, I'm struggling to keep the lies straight. But you know I'm just floating around, half-scared that I'll be untethered any moment but desperately wanting to anyway."

"You want to fly, *cara*?"

"Like you couldn't imagine. Nothing worse than fear that keeps you still."

He watched her for a long beat. Then, as if all her raw vulnerability meant nothing, he grabbed a cold washcloth and pressed it against her face.

His fingers were so refreshingly gentle as he wiped away the sticky remnants of the orange juice from her temples and her hair.

Sam closed her eyes and let the sensations take hold. In a delicious contrast, his warm breath coasted over her skin.

Her spine felt like it was made of those chocolate

straws her mom used to buy for Sam to drink her milk with—melting and bendy at his fingers.

With an efficiency that made her smile, he wiped down her cheek and neck. Suddenly, his fingers were at the buttons of her shirt dress. Her eyes flying open, he gripped his wrist.

Jaw tight, he said, "There's more on your neck."

Sam did feel the stickiness between her breasts. "I'll just shower—"

The first button on the shirt popped off. Two more buttons and he would see the scar that was a reminder of how she'd spent her teens. He'd already been avoiding her for the past week. Panic gripped her. "Stop unbuttoning my dress."

He arched a brow, his fingers lingering over the third button. "Why am I not surprised that you're a prude, *bella*?"

"Of course I'm not," she said with a forced laugh. "Just because I don't want to get half-naked in the kitchen."

"Let me carry you to the bedroom, then."

"I can walk—"

"I feel responsible for—"

Sam clasped his jaw. "Alessandro, I don't need your fucking pity."

His fingers lingered on the third button of her shirt. The patch of her bare skin where he touched her burned. "The last thing I feel when I look at you is pity, *tesoro*."

"And yet I'm so easy to avoid, so forgettable, *si*?"

His gaze met hers and held, his fury slowly cycling out and replaced with something else. Long fingers touched her jaw, his grip tender. "You're the least forgettable woman I've ever met. Ever since you…" His exhale was long. The thrust of his fingers through his hair rough, his words gravelly. "What do you want of me, Sam?"

Sam leaned forward and pressed her mouth to his cheek. Her heart beat so rapidly in her chest that it should've scared her, but sitting in the warm cocoon of his body, she felt so vibrantly alive that there was no place for fear.

Hands gripping her shoulders, he went utterly rigid.

"One kiss," she said, the stubble on his chin scraping her lips in an abrasive whisper. "So that I know how you taste. So that I know you want me. One kiss, Alessandro, so that I can live it a million times in my head." Her breath left her in a shuddering exhale as she waited.

All her life, she'd waited for others to make life-changing, sometimes life-threatening decisions for her. From doctors to her parents to the universe, her will nothing but a swaying leaf in a storm. But this waiting…there was pleasure in this.

This was a battle. Her will against his, her need against his control. Ordinary, dull, unexciting Sam against remote, ruthless, strikingly beautiful Alessandro Ricci.

This was a waiting she'd plunge herself into again and again. A choice she would make a thousand times.

If all of her entire being weren't tuned in to him, Sam wouldn't have sensed it. But he moved, and his mouth shifted until it sat flush against hers. A dam of longing, never too far beneath surface, broke through her.

His mouth—oh, his mouth!—was soft and firm as she moved her lips. The man was full of contradictions, and she liked every bit of him. Up and down, messy and damp and a little rough, she rubbed her lips against his, every minuscule motion sending a shocking jolt of molten heat to her sex. Then she licked his lower lip and nipped it.

She stretched her thighs wider so that she could scoot closer, so that she could feel of all him against her. And he let her. Not for a second was Sam unaware that he was granting her this. That his own control was hanging by a thread, that she desperately needed to snap it.

A long, shuddering sigh left her as her chest grazed his, as her belly pressed against his hard one and their hips flushed. She couldn't help but thrust her hips, a soft gasp escaping her. Slowly, every cell in her came awake with a blistering heat as his arousal took shape and form against her core, as it lengthened. The very thought of that hard length inside her made her sex clench greedily.

His curse punctured the silence as loudly as if the bright chandelier overhead had crashed into a million pieces around them. But all Sam cared about was the warmth unspooling in her lower belly, untethering her.

She had done this to him—naïve, unsophisticated, unexciting Sam. Confidence and desire whipped through her, an explosive cocktail. Tightening her fingers at the nape of his neck, she kissed him again.

She traced the shape of those thin lips with the tip of her tongue, nipped at the lower lip with her teeth, licked at him like a lazy cat until he opened to her with a guttural groan that set off vibrations through her. Greedy for more, she licked into his mouth, stroking, tasting, teasing, taunting, stealing his breath for herself.

A rough growl escaped him as his hand wrapped around the nape of her neck. Sam groaned as he bent her back over his arm, and then his mouth devoured her. She finally understood what those flashes of consuming hunger in his eyes meant. There was no sweet exploration, no soft learning.

Alessandro ravished her. He took from her as if she were the last breath of air. Drank from her lips as if she were the last sip of water.

Pleasure flew through her in rivulets, pooling at her sex into damp readiness. The kiss was all him—the licking fire of hard nips, the cooling ice of soothing licks—a spectrum of pain and pleasure in between.

No safety, no soft whispers, only sheer hunger. Within moments, he taught her how to deepen the pleasure blooming between them, when to pull away and when to cling.

His hands moved all over her hips and back and spine and neck and butt, coasting, kneading, touching, learning. Provoking and soothing. Owning. His touch was full of a possessive intent that made her want to submit to everything he did. For every hurt he caused with those teeth, he gave back pleasure that resonated a thousand times more deeply.

Sam groaned into his mouth, the thrust of his hips making his erection hit her exactly where she needed. She locked her legs around his hips, brazenly thrusting against him. Hands fisted in his shirt, she was sobbing, begging for more, begging him for relief.

When he trailed a path over her jaw and neck, she buried her hands in his hair, her body a mass of sensations she couldn't catalog fast enough. But it was her heart that felt full to bursting. Her heart's unfathomable desire for more that terrified her.

"Is this enough to prove I want you, *tesoro*? That I lose control when anyone could walk in?"

If he'd mocked her, maybe Sam could have pulled her senses out of the miasma of longing. But there was no humor in his words. Nothing but a deep hunger for more that she recognized in herself.

She looked up at him, fighting the pull of reality. Fighting the embarrassed heat that was already flowing into her cheeks. "Have *you* had enough?"

One corded arm swung around her lower back, and he pulled her forward.

A filthy curse and a string of Italian met her ears when she thrust up in answer. Then his mouth touched hers in a sweet kiss that stole the breath from her lungs. Wedged hard against him, the heat and hardness of his erection branded her. All she wanted was to move, to rub up against him until the restlessness under her skin found a destination. But his grip was firm on her legs, keeping her prisoner.

"From the moment I saw you, standing apart from the crowd…"

Sam wanted to ask what he was talking about. But he didn't give her a chance.

His mouth and his whispers and his kisses stole rational thought. "Wanting something so much, only…" He drew a trail from the corner of her mouth to her chin to the pulse at her neck, punctuating his kisses with words, breathing them into her skin.

And then suddenly, he stopped.

She sensed the shift in his mood as easily as if someone had dumped a bucket of ice-cold water over them. "Alessandro," she whispered, pushing that one lock of unruly hair from his forehead like she'd wanted to so many times. "What is it?"

He didn't budge. Didn't look up.

Slowly, he pulled the flaps of the dress apart. And Sam knew what had stopped his lazy exploration. What had frozen him.

Alessandro stared blankly, his stomach so tight with lust that it took him a few minutes to circle back to what had made him stop.

He had ripped the rest of the buttons until her ridiculous dress had fallen open, baring her chest and belly to him. The clingy material cupped her small breasts, and his palms ached to do the same.

She wasn't wearing a bra. The edges of the dress just barely covered the tight knots of her nipples. He could see the light brown aureoles, the tips pushing at the fabric.

He'd also pushed the dress up her thighs, which were stretched wide. Her skin was silky smooth. Lips swollen, hair half out of her braid, she was the most achingly lovely thing Alessandro had ever seen. So lovely that the image of her like this would haunt him for the rest of his life.

All he wanted to do was bend his head and lick her all over. Up and down, around the swells of her breasts and below, until he could play with her piercing.

It took him an eternity to focus on the scar he'd felt under his fingertips. For a second, he'd thought he'd imagined it and stepped back.

Sunlight illuminated her golden-brown skin and the rough ridge of the scar drew a line down, starting at the top between her breasts, going lower. Deep too, as if someone had taken a scalpel and dug into her flesh not just once but multiple times.

He traced it up and down, fighting for control over his breath. Fighting to not give into the panic inching its fingers all across him, leaving something cold and ugly in its trail. Breath harsh, he pressed his palm against her rib cage, desperate to feel the beat of her heart. The thud of it, the soft gasp from her lips, made him realize how roughly he'd grabbed her. He jerked away, feeling as if he'd been hit in the head and it was still ringing.

Her throat bobbed, sending a ripple of motion down her chest, and his gaze jerked up to meet hers. For once, he couldn't read her expression. Always so open and honest and artlessly direct—her words and her eyes. Yet now, it was as if she'd slammed a shutter down between them.

He traced the scar gently, unable to stop. "What... made this?"

"Heart surgery."

A quiet roar reverberated within him, demanding release. "When?"

"What do you mean, when?"

"When did you have the surgery, Sameera?" he bit out.

"I had three heart surgeries between ages eleven and eighteen. The third time was due to a valve problem." There was a forced lightness to her words that he knew was fake. It was probably the first time he'd seen her fake anything. "But I've enjoyed perfect health ever since the last one."

Her words were soft as if she was determined to manage his mood, manage him.

A part of him, the rational part, warned that she shouldn't have to manage his emotions when she revealed such private information. That the onus of his reaction shouldn't be on her. And yet, he couldn't pin his emotions down, couldn't shove them away so that he didn't discomfit her.

"That's where you met Matteo," he said tonelessly, remembering Matteo going to see their great-aunt who lived in California when she'd had surgery. "At the hospital."

"In the hospital café, while I was still in my horrible ass-baring gown." Her wide smile was the genuine thing. "I'd snuck away from my ward. Bored out of my mind because they said I should stay overnight for a routine checkup. I wanted chips. But I forgot cash. He bought me a bag of chips and flirted with me outrageously right there, while I tried not to flash him my ass."

Emotion rattled him—thick and blinding, familiarly unfamiliar, bringing images to bore down on him like an avalanche. The very thought of Sameera looking small and tiny on a clinical hospital bed stole his breath.

The image was too vivid. Too real.

He'd seen Violetta like that for so long. For four years, he'd spent hours at her side in the evenings, reading to her, playing chess with her, holding her hand.

It was diabolically cruel how easily his mind replaced Violetta with Sam... Sam in an ugly pristine white hospital. Sam with her smile faint, the light in her eyes dim. Sam with her breath thin and faint.

Maledizione! He pushed away from the table, sweat beading on his face. His mind was playing games. Triggering memories from a painful period in his life. Which was ridiculous.

Yes, Sam had reminded him of Violetta from the first. Something about the glowing spirit wrapped in steel that they possessed. But Violetta was gone. And Sam was here, vibrantly alive.

"Alessandro?"

He turned to find Sam watching him with trepidation in her eyes.

"That's why your parents are so protective of you." Everything fell into place, but he'd never wanted more to live in ignorance, had never understood Matteo's love for deluding himself more. "Why you still live with them. Why…" His words became sharp, hostile. "Why didn't you tell me?"

"Why would I?" she asked in a small, baffled voice.

It was like waving a red flag in front of an angry bull. "I asked you point-blank why they were so protective of you."

"So?" Anger painted her cheeks a reddish tint. "I didn't have to share anything with you. Especially now, when you're actively avoiding me." She pushed off from the table, her dress still unbuttoned to her belly button. Her hair was in a disarray, her neck and jaw a little reddened where his stubble had scratched her. She looked glorious. "You think I walk around showing people my scar and telling them my history?"

"Why is that wrong? What if you needed an emergency visit? How was I supposed to take care of you? How can you be so irresponsible and flippant about this?"

She flinched, and Alessandro wondered if he was losing his mind.

Chin quivering, she looked at him as if he'd betrayed her in the worst possible way. "I'm choosing to see this as your concern for me and not…" Her words shook, slender body trembling with fury. "If you ever assume that I don't know my own mind or even insinuate that I'm helpless… I'll never forgive you." She swallowed, and that she had a better measure of control over her emotions than he did right then shamed him. "I have all my insurance information, my medication prescriptions, my monthly checkups already set up. As for emergency, it's no different from anyone else needing to be rushed to the ER."

"I still think you should've shared your—"

"Why? So that everyone can look at me the way you're looking at me now? I can see the way you perceive me shifting in front of my very eyes…" Her words held a question in them.

But Alessandro couldn't think beyond what it meant to him. Couldn't get perspective. Silence had never felt like it could tear two people apart.

Hurt twisted her smile into a mockery. "Thinking this thing between us was worthy of exploration was a colossal mistake. My age, Matteo, and now my history…you'll find something to reject this. And that's your prerogative. But I'll be damned if I let you make me believe that I'm not—" Tears filled her eyes and she inhaled loudly. "I finally understand why Matteo calls you a machine. But he doesn't know the worst, does he? It's not that you can't feel. It's that you don't want to."

She swept out of the kitchen, holding her dress together, her spine straight, head held high.

Alessandro stayed still for a long time, his mind still reeling. Suddenly, he could see all the reasons their chemistry was more than surface level: because she understood what it meant to not have power over your own life.

But her fears and her very real struggles hadn't

stopped her from wanting to live, from wanting to taste everything life offered. From recognizing the same hunger in him, even though he was everything she called him—remote, ruthless, heartless.

Only now did he realize how much more he'd lost than Violetta fourteen years ago. Grief had robbed so much from him—friends, of family, even his brother. Laughter. Simple pleasures. The ability to connect.

It had isolated him until he had gotten used to having nothing.

CHAPTER EIGHT

MORE THAN A week passed before Alessandro went to visit an awake Matteo.

While his brother had been conscious for over two weeks now, he had avoided seeing him. Now his stomach tightened at the prospect of a confrontation that had been coming for months, even years.

Neither did he miss the fact that the trigger was Sam's arrival.

It had been a week since Sam had looked at him with such anger, such hurt in her eyes. The first he could bear, the second not so much.

"Where is she?" he said, barging into the room. "Don't pretend ignorance, Matteo. She doesn't know anyone in this town."

His chest tightened at the sight of his brother. Dark, sunken shadows clung to Matteo's eyes, the ever-present pain already changing the cast of his features.

"Hello to you too, Alessandro," Matteo said. "If you mean Angelina, she's not here. Because you banished her." He sighed. "Aren't you the one always telling me to not piss off Vittorio?"

"I meant Sam, and you know it," Alessandro countered. His words sharpened in direct reaction to how pale and worn-out Matteo looked. It seemed his usual self-possession was nowhere to be found now. "But while we're talking about Angelina, have you finally decided to be a responsible adult and sort this mess out? Will you stop overcompensating for your supposed weaknesses as a child and act like a grown-up instead?"

"*Sì*, something shook loose in my brain during the accident," his brother said, shutting Alessandro up.

Whatever he had been expecting, it wasn't Matteo's sudden somberness. Alessandro felt as if he'd kicked a dog that was already down.

"You should know that I told Angelina everything over the phone. How Sam hadn't yet quite broken up with me when I agreed to go out with her. But that I knew it was coming. That I went out with Angelina to feel better about myself."

"At least you can be glad there's nothing else to break in your body. Not everyone is as forgiving as Sam." It was a big step for his brother to admit how far down the wrong path he'd gone. Fresh anger surged through Alessandro. "Before you decided to come clean, did you think about Sam's safety? Did you not realize Angelina would take it out on her?"

"You have no idea how sorry I am. How awful Angelina feels about her behavior toward Sam." When Alessandro scoffed, Matteo sighed. "No, truly. She hasn't told her cousins or friends or her dad everything I told her about Sam and me. She said it wasn't anyone's business."

For once, Alessandro was surprised too.

Matteo bumped his head against the headboard. "The last thing I want is to hurt Sam more. She's...special."

Hearing her name on his brother's lips made Alessandro want to smash something. Even if she wasn't for him. "Are you still in love with her?"

"I used to think so," Matteo answered, his voice steady. "But when I realized she didn't feel deeply about me, that she'd already outgrown me, it made me resentful. I knew then that our relationship was more about how she made me feel about myself, rather than our feelings for each other."

"Because of her...history?"

"Sam made me feel good in my own skin," Matteo said, regret and something else in his eyes. "As if I were a different kind of man. Like I could be someone even without the Ricci name or the large sphere of your influence. If a fearless girl like her could love me, I was worthy. I never told her about our family wealth because I wanted a girl like her to like me for me...without complications. And her parents were too protective of her to ever let her travel, so...she never saw all of this for herself."

As much as he hated it, Alessandro understood the sentiment. "Is that why you never told us that Sam was a woman? Because you wanted to keep her and our family separate?"

"*Sì*. Even when it was good, I knew it wouldn't last, that it wouldn't survive in the true reality of my world. And Sam hasn't looked at me like I was her hero in a long while."

"And Angelina?" demanded Alessandro.

"Angelina's not ready to call it quits. For now, she's claiming that if she breaks up with me, society will think she's dumping me because I'm not the dynamic, charming prize she wanted in the first place. I think she wants to see who I am beneath the bravado. I'm afraid to tell her I might be nothing."

"Don't say that." Alessandro reached for his brother's hand, swallowing past the ache in his throat. "When I saw you in the hospital bed, I realized I had let small resentments fester. I'm sorry I never told you that I care about you."

Vulnerability shone in his brother's eyes. "I never gave you a reason to. The more you warned me about the consequences of my lifestyle, the worse I behaved." Hope danced in his face. "I will do better, Alessandro. As soon as I have mobility, I plan to start work. Believe it or not, my degree in accounting can be put to some use." He raised a hand, forestalling Alessandro. "I already spoke to Papà. I'll start as a junior clerk in the accounts department and work my way up. I will prove you wrong."

"Apparently, it's been a month of me being proved wrong."

Matteo regarded him thoughtfully. "Are we going to talk about Sam and you?"

"That's none of your—" Alessandro pushed his hand through his hair and blew out a breath. "No."

"So there is something between you two." For a second, old bitterness flashed in his brother's eyes, and Alessandro braced himself. Matteo's mouth twisted ruefully. "I could see it even that first night in your study, the way you looked at each other. It made me…" He shook his head, dislodging his curls onto his forehead.

While the last thing he wanted was to discuss Sam with his brother, Alessandro waited. Matteo needed this. Especially if they meant to begin their relationship anew.

"She's honest enough to admit that you shut it down

before it even began," Matteo said finally. "I thought I'd be happy. As much as it's a bitter pill to swallow that she prefers you, I can see you…feel something for her too."

"As much as I appreciate your blessing," Alessandro bared his teeth in a mockery of smile, "I want you to tell me her whereabouts right now."

Matteo sighed. "Sam said she wanted to go out. Angelina took her to a club."

Alessandro scowled. "Angelina threw a glass of juice in Sam's face not two days ago."

"She apologized, and Sam forgave her." Mateo held up his phone, eyes twinkling. "Do you want to see the pics Angelina's been sending me all evening?"

He took the phone from his brother and looked at the screen.

It was a picture of Sam against the bright lights of the nightclub. In a strapless dress in a shiny material in a rainbow of colors, the asymmetrical strips hugging her torso. It cupped her chest loosely, baring the lush swells in a provocative way that made hunger tighten his muscles. But it was the scar that held his interest.

All these weeks, she'd worn dresses and tops that buttoned up all the way.

Yet, now she showed off the scar proudly, even loudly. He wanted to think that he'd brought that change in her, but that was arrogance talking. Sam was only beginning to own herself.

"Swipe through. There's more," Matteo added.

Alessandro swiped. There were numerous pictures and even video clips—Sam laughing, singing at the top of her voice, swinging her hips. Sam sandwiched between two guys while a slow jazz tune played in the background.

Jealousy and something much darker scoured through him in hot trails, making his stomach tighten. He threw the phone back to the bed.

As he walked out, Matteo said, "Sam deserves the best."

Did Matteo think he didn't know that?

She was happy, Alessandro told himself, reaching for the decanter of bourbon in his study. She was twenty-three, and she was doing things people of her age did.

He told himself that again and again as he called his sparring partner Bruno. If what he needed was to have it beaten into him that he should leave Sam alone, then that's what he would do.

She didn't need to say good-bye.

But as Sam walked around his study, the only room in the house that reflected Alessandro's personality, she admitted to herself that she didn't want to leave without seeing him. Not after all the days she'd spent taking over his bedroom. Not after everything he'd done, in his own way, to watch out for her. Not after everything they'd shared.

He'd hurt her, and the worst part was that she'd thought he was one man who never would. She'd foolishly assumed that he liked her for who she was. Maybe she was nothing more to him than his younger brother's foolish, naïve ex who wouldn't leave.

She'd walked into the study after Angelina had dropped her off. The very woman she'd been loath to meet from that first evening had now become a good friend. Angelina was a spoiled diva with an explosive temper, but beneath it all she was just like Sam: full of insecurities and flaws and desires.

Now that she had Angelina's offer of accommodation at her cousin's place, she needn't stay at the villa at all. It was late, but once the offer had been made, Sam knew she needed to leave immediately.

For the first time in her life, she'd gone clubbing with friends. She'd danced. She'd sung at the top of her lungs. She'd ingested secondhand smoke. She'd flirted. While none of the guys had made her heart flutter like the heartless man who belonged here, it felt good to know that someone did want her.

Smiling, she poured herself a finger of Scotch. She lifted the glass to her mouth when a rough hand pulled the drink away from her and ended up sloshing it all over her. "Jesus Christ! Enough with spilling my drinks."

"What the hell do you think you're doing?" Alessandro glared at her.

A soft gasp escaped her mouth.

His face was…a kaleidoscope of bruises. The lower lip she was so obsessed with was swollen and cut with crusted blood. A cut under his right eye made his cheekbone swell up, and a blue-green bruise the size of her palm painted his jaw. This was so far from the calm, remote Alessandro she'd known from day one that she forgot her anger. "Are you in pain?"

Leaning against the desk, he threw his legs forward. "Pain was the point of it."

"You look like you took part in a street fight. And lost."

"Ahh, your lack of faith hurts more than all of this, *tesoro*. I promise Bruno looks worse than me."

She rubbed her palms over her hips, just to do something. "I thought you were beyond all this, your control ironclad."

His gaze searched her face and held hers. "I was in a nasty mood, and there were only two ways to work it out of my system."

Heat flushed through her in warm rivulets at his tone.

"What were *you* about to do? Alcohol messes with your medication."

Back to this, were they? "Two sips won't kill me."

He raised a brow, and even with his face all bruised, it was the most arrogant gesture she'd ever seen. It made her blood boil, brought all the anger and hurt back to the surface. Looking away, she grabbed her jacket from the desk. "I was stupid enough to want to say good-bye."

"Good-bye?"

She reached the damned heavy double doors. "I'm leaving."

He stalked toward her. There was no other word for it. "And going where exactly?"

Sam took him in—how the drop of blood on the pristine white of his shirt looked so out of place, the buttons undone to his abdomen showing olive skin sprinkled with sparse chest hair, how his usually immaculate black trousers were rumpled. How he hadn't even waited long enough to change before sparring.

As if all the masks of politeness had been stripped off, leaving him with only pure instincts and wants.

She wanted him even more like this. Wanted this raw, distilled version of Alessandro to want her.

"Angelina's cousin's apartment. I'll still visit Matteo

daily. Angelina knows the truth. There's no need for us to pretend."

"Did you have fun at the club?"

The sudden switch in the conversation left her unbalanced. "I did." She didn't even have to force the smile. "Angelina's cousins are a hoot. Especially after she told them that I'd never been to a club before. Had never danced before, never been flirted with before." The twins had been outrageous to begin with, sandwiching her between them on the dance floor, but it was harmless fun.

"Did you like all the attention you got?" There it was again, that feral quality about him. Somehow, he'd stalked her back across the room until she was leaning against his desk. Away from the door. "Did you dance with those two men to make me jealous, Sam?"

"I don't play games like that." She frowned. "Wait, how did you know I was dancing with…" She bit her lip, and his gaze zoomed down. Heat crested her cheeks as she remembered all the crazy things she'd gotten up to. "You saw those videos?"

"Matteo showed them to me."

Whether he knew it or not, he'd pushed her into crawling out of her shell. Into owning her scar and her body.

She'd been terrified when she'd walked into the club. Terrified that her scar would be the only thing people would see, that it'd make them feel sorry for her. But while one of Angelina's girlfriends had openly asked her about it, no one had given it a second glance.

While she was never going to be comfortable in provocative clothes, now she knew that it was her choice. Not one made out of shame.

"You won't make me feel guilty about it. Not about

this overtly provocative dress. Not about the secondhand smoke I inhaled. Not about the fact that I enjoyed flirting with two men. Men of my age. Men who found me sexy and interesting."

He cast a long look at the dress in question, his lashes flicking down. But his gaze didn't linger on her scar. It moved over the upper swells of her breasts, the asymmetric hem that barely covered her left thigh and her feet clad in black stilettos. Then it climbed back up over her, and this time it did linger on her scar.

Long fingers clasped her cheek with such gentle reverence that all the longing she'd fought flooded back into her. "Tell me why you want to leave."

"I don't want to let one arrogant asshole's rejection ruin my trip."

He laughed, a deep, hard sound that enveloped her. And then he hissed in pain. The cut in his lower lip had split again, and a drop of blood appeared.

She pressed the pad of her thumb to stanch it. He flinched but held still. "I didn't mean to hurt you more," she whispered, a languid heat spreading through her.

He clasped her wrist and pressed his face into her palm. His body caged hers against the desk without quite touching. "I like all the things you inflict on me, *bella*. Laughter, hurt, jealousy… They remind me that I'm alive." He nuzzled into the side of her face. His chest rose and fell, the tension in his body setting hers alight. "You've no idea how much I loathe myself for hurting you."

The soft press of his lips at her temple cracked open her heart with such violence that Sam couldn't breathe. Word by word, kiss by kiss, he was stealing away parts of her, and she didn't know how to keep herself intact anymore.

"Then, don't," she whispered, tucking her chin into the crook of his elbow. He smelled of sweat and blood and whiskey, and she inhaled him as if he were air. Fingers around his forearm, she clung to him, loving the fierce heat of his body.

"I haven't felt anything for so long... With you, it is futile to resist." His soft words were breathed into her skin, as if he were releasing the shackles around himself. He tilted her chin up. "Tell me what hurt you so much."

"You looked at me as if I was...broken. As if my history makes me damaged. Even Matteo behaved better."

He was shaking his head, regret making his face even more severe. "Ahh...you know just how to hurt me."

Sam shook her head. "I—"

Thumb notching into her chin, he cut her off. "Look at me, Sameera. Listen to me." His warm breath feathered over her face. "In my eyes, you're perfection. From the moment you walked in, I wished you were mine. I burn with jealousy when you talk of him with such fondness. How I reacted...it's my weakness, *bella*. Not you."

His hands cradled her head, and his mouth hovered an inch over her mouth, and Sam thought she might be drowning but she didn't care. "I want you so much, Sam, it's an ache in my body. Even the bruises won't kill it. But the thing is..." he licked her lower lip, and a hot poker of sensation hit her "... I can't offer anything beyond a few weeks. No future, no relationship. This would be an affair to work you out of my system. For some goddamned reason, you're a novelty. But the fascination will wear off."

"How does your brutal honesty make you hotter?" she

said, chasing his lips. She licked his lower lip, tasted the blood and then nipped him right where the lip was split.

He shuddered, jerked her toward him until she wrapped her arms around his neck and every inch of her was plastered to him. "All I have to give you is pleasure. But you're the kind of girl—"

Sam buried her face in the hollow at his throat and scraped her teeth over his pulse. "I'm the kind of woman who has filthy dreams about you, Alessandro. The kind that wanted you from the first moment, even though I came here for Mateo. The kind of woman who touches herself thinking of you. The kind of woman who survived three surgeries as a teenager and wants to taste life. If you hated hurting me, then make it better. Make me feel good."

"*Bene.*" He licked the shell of her ear, and Sam shivered. Then his mouth went south, trailing warm, wet kisses across her neck, her shoulders, the swell of her breasts.

She swept her hands over him, the sharp jut of his shoulders, the warm, taut skin of his chest, the hard muscles beneath. That she could touch him with such abandon made her breath falter. She snuck her fingers under his shirt, scoring his abdomen with her nails, then trailed them lower.

"No." His forbidding tone made her belly roll. "My control is so thin, *tesoro*. And my need to be inside you... too high."

"Yes."

Gripping her wrists with one hand, he pushed them above her head with a growl that made dampness gush at her sex. "I want to make it up to you. I want you to forget the men you were dancing with, the ones you flirted with. I want you screaming my name."

Sam twisted, trying to throw off his hold. She felt a soft breeze on her bare breasts before she heard the hiss of the zipper on her dress. Her nipples instantly puckered, brazenly begging.

"Perfection," he whispered, gray eyes heavy with desire.

He watched her as he cupped them. As he swirled mindless circles around her nipples. As he rubbed the aching buds with his fingers. As he played with her relentlessly until her spine was bowing toward him. As he bent his head and flicked at one aching bud and then… feasted on her.

It was greedy and dirty and wet, and she was bent over his arm as he licked and nipped and drew her into the wet cavern of his mouth. Need pooled low, making her thong damp.

She moaned in protest when he released her, afraid he was abandoning her again. Until firm fingers clasped her calves.

Heart fluttering behind her rib cage like a trapped bird, Sam looked down.

He was kneeling between her thighs, his face tilted up. Elegant hands pulled her thighs until her ass was half hanging off the desk. And then for long, breathtaking moments he watched her—from her hair spilling over her bare shoulders, her knotted nipples wet from his mouth, the diamond glinting at her belly button, to her hips where her dress pooled.

His nostrils flared, and there was a harsh, saturnine quality to his expression that made the hunger in his eyes seem devouring. "I wish you could see yourself now. As I see you, Sameera. You'd never doubt what I think of you, then." The gravelly edge of his voice at the end said something she couldn't catch. "Spread your thighs."

"What?" Heat crawled up her bare chest, up her neck until it crested in her cheeks.

"I want to taste you."

"But...you didn't even kiss me." She groaned inwardly. Could she sound more like a high-school girl with a crush on him?

He raised a brow. That damned brow was going to be the death of her.

He was on his knees in front of her, a position she was sure no one saw Alessandro Ricci in. His face was blue and green with bruises, his lower lip split. His hair messed up by her fingers. And yet he looked like he owned the world. Like he owned this room. Like he owned her.

"You're not comfortable with this?" His palms crawled up her calves, caressed her shins, cupped her knees, stroked the lines that connected her thighs and hips.

Sam flushed. He had to know she was dripping wet. He was showing her how this was going to play out between them. Not with soft whispers. No endearments. No sweet promises. This would be purely sexual. If he thought she'd back down, he didn't know her. "I have a question for you."

"Wondering if it will feel good?"

Alessandro didn't know what devil was goading him. It was clear from her face that he was going far too fast for her. That for all her defiant acceptance of his terms, she was young and had had one boyfriend. Which he couldn't even bear to think of.

He had to keep the boundaries clear in his own head, though. Had to keep this physical. He knew he could never allow himself love again, not after the loss he felt with Violetta.

"I already know it will feel amazing," she said, such trust in her eyes. "Are you doing it to prove something?"

"Ever since you walked in and said I was not..." He didn't want to hear his brother's name in this space between them. Not even on his own lips. He wanted no one in this space between them. "You're not the only one with filthy dreams, *bella*."

Her gaze glittered, as if he'd given her a priceless gift, and her hard swallow sent motion rippling down her chest. Eyes locked with his, she fisted her dress in one hand. The pulse at her neck quivered. Ever so slowly, she lifted her foot, placed it on his shoulder and bent her knee until she was all open for him. A flimsy thong, already damp, barely hid her from him.

Lust and tenderness warred within him, rioting out of control. He was never going to walk into this room and not see her sitting at the desk like this.

A little nervous, eyes darkened, brazenly open for his pleasure. *All his.*

He pressed her inner thighs obscenely wide until his shoulders were wedged under her knees and he buried his face in her mound. She jerked and groaned and buried her fingers in his hair when he notched his nose into her folds and breathed her scent in.

His erection throbbed with a life of its own, his muscles, already bruised and beaten, begging for release.

One hard tug ripped the thong off. Looking up, he let her see his rampant desire as he slowly traced the shape of her folds. "I knew you would be pretty all over. But how eagerly you drip for me..." Holding her gaze, he licked at the tip of one finger and made a humming sound at the back of his throat. "You taste divine."

"You still owe me a kiss," she whispered, her fingers sifting through his hair.

"After," he said, grinning. Under his fingers, her core fluttered. He rubbed his fingers up and down, and all around, without touching her clit. "When my mouth is full of your arousal. Then you can taste yourself on my lips."

Her spine arched into his touch, her hips doing the same. Color high in her cheeks, she dug her teeth into her lower lip. Her small breasts rose and fell with her shallow pants, the tight knots of her nipples beckoning for more. "Why didn't I guess that you would go slow enough that I'd expire from waiting?"

"What do you want, Sam?"

"I want to come. So hard that I black out. So hard that reality beats my dreams of you."

"That I can manage," he said and slowly penetrated her with one finger. She swallowed him like a vise, making his cock throb painfully. He cursed and worked in another finger. "You're so wet and tight for me. I can't wait to bury myself inside you, *bella*."

A hoarse mewl tore out of Sam's mouth. While she adjusted to the intrusion, he draped her wetness all over, up and down, teasing, stroking, building her up.

Her fingers in his hair tugged jerkily. He smiled

against her inner thigh and nipped the sensitive skin. Her hips thrust forward, the muscles in her thighs tense and taut.

Burying his smile in her sex, Alessandro took a lick of her. Lingered with his tongue pressed against her opening. Sucked at the dampness.

Arching into his touch, she breathed out in rough pants.

He laved her with his tongue, but he didn't touch her clit yet. Not until her legs were locked over his upper back.

His name on her lips rang around, a soft litany, a harsh curse, begging for benediction. Every time she got to the edge, he retreated, soothed her, played with her. His erection pressed painfully against his trousers.

She was honey-sweet on his tongue, tart like grapes and an aphrodisiac like he'd never known. He'd only done this for one other woman in his life. The memory slammed into him. After she'd read it in some magazine and demanded it of him. He'd done it because he wanted something in return from her.

But with Sam, he'd wanted to from the first moment. Not just this—he wanted to do every thing he'd ever imagined to her. He wanted to mark her, inside and out, so that she'd never forget him. So that she never went to another man and didn't think of him.

A hard tug in his hair had him looking up. Her breasts heaved, her nipples all plump and pretty. And her eyes… dilated and full of a raw hunger for him.

Alessandro reached up with one hand and traced the scar, a strange hollow in his stomach.

"Please, Alessandro, no more…"

He tweaked one nipple, and she arched into the touch. "No more of this, *bella*?"

She cursed. "No more tormenting me."

"That's up to me, *tesoro*." He hooked the fingers inside her and pressed at the soft spot. Her mouth fell open on a guttural moan.

He watched her, his heartbeat thundering, every inch of him taut.

But when she looked at him, there was something in her eyes that speared him in his chest. "You promised me pleasure."

He latched onto her clit with his lips and sucked.

She fell apart in seconds, her fingers scratching and digging into his neck, her sex contracting around his fingers, her hips chasing his mouth in an erotic tango. A soft cry fell from her lips as another climax followed the first.

When he pushed to his feet, she folded into his embrace—damp and soft and trembling—her arms thrown about his waist, face hidden in his chest. Her tears seeped through the shirt into his skin.

He pushed away damp tendrils from her forehead, tenderness engulfing him. "Sam?"

"Don't look at me. I'm just being naïve and silly."

"Take as long as you want, *bella*."

Gathering her to him, he held her, an indescribable sensation cracking open in his chest. This was no affair he would walk away from unscathed. This woman was doing something to him, and he had no defenses left. No willpower to fight.

"Damn, you're good at that," she whispered, before looking up.

"You're vocal and responsive and greedy," he said, tweaking her nose. "That makes you the perfect lover."

"That is high praise. Just don't expect the same kind of expertise from me, okay? I've barely scratched the—" she pressed a hand to her mouth, her eyes suddenly wary.

The last thing he wanted was a look into past lovers. It didn't matter if it was Matteo or someone else. Even the idea of another man seeing her laughter, her tears, her vulnerability threatened to reduce him into nothing but animal instincts.

"You don't have much experience," he said, with a grumbling sigh. "Shall we leave it at that?"

The wariness fled, and laughter danced in her eyes. "How are you hot even when you're so disgruntled and grumpy?"

He kissed her softly, slowly. She licked his lower lip, brown eyes shimmering. "I want to go down on you."

His cock twitched in his trousers. "Not tonight."

"Why do you get to make the rules?"

"Because I'm an arrogant asshole, and I want things the way I want them. When I want them."

She scrunched her nose at him. "Then, we're going to spend my stay fighting and not f—"

With one quick tug, he had her over his shoulder and made for the dark corridor that led to his bedroom. "So you *are* staying with me, then," he said. "I'm glad I've persuaded you."

She squealed and thumped his back. Sudden fear thrummed through him when she panted roughly. "Sameera, is this okay?"

She stilled for a second, then sighed. "Except for the fact that I'm enjoying being carried around like a sack of potatoes far too much for a modern twenty-first-century woman, yes. The view of your ass is particularly spectacular from here."

He tensed but asked anyway. "Will you tell me immediately if at any time you feel...different?" His fingers gripped the backs of her upper thighs.

Her hesitation pricked him. How did he explain to her that his protectiveness didn't mean he thought less of her when he didn't understand it himself? When he wanted to wrap her in a cocoon and never let her out of his sight? She'd surely hate him then.

"Yes, I'll let you know if I feel unwell. Would you like to know the signs to watch out for?" she said after what felt like an eternity.

"Sì."

"Migraine. Pallor. Light-headedness."

Relief shuddered through him. "Thank you for telling me."

Her hands moved over his back, stroking, kneading. Then she giggled. "FYI, breathlessness after an arrogant Italian expertly eats me out is not a danger sign. Please keep the orgasms coming."

His laughter echoed in the dark, and he ran his right palm up and down her leg. She nuzzled her face into his back in a gesture of affection that made him dizzy.

The corridor felt like a different reality, one which he didn't want to emerge from. He was smiling in the dark like a fool, and his chest felt lighter, his limbs looser than he'd felt in...forever.

She sighed. And he wondered if she felt the same sense of lightness he did. "Is this flying, Alessandro?"

"No, *tesoro*."

"Then, maybe I'm dead? Because so much pleasure should have killed me."

He pushed the silky hem of her dress aside and smacked her bare ass lightly. "That's not funny," he bit out. Filthy, greedy man that he was, though, he let his fingers linger over the curve of her ass.

Her outraged gasp shivered down his spine. "Okay, that's not a kink I'm into."

"And what if I was?"

With a growl, the minx grabbed his back and pushed herself up. Her teeth dug into his upper shoulder. *Hard.* As a direct reaction, his cock was so hard now it was uncomfortable to walk. "Something like that work?"

"Maybe," he said, grinning.

Every time he'd imagined them together like this, he'd known it would be new. Different because of everything she inevitably forced him to feel. Passionate. Hot. But this...

He grunted when she bit him again, switched his palm to the other cheek, delivered another tap on her ass, and then while she was biting and cursing him, he walked into his bedroom. Which she'd completely made hers.

He threw her on his bed and climbed over her. Her complaints, her kisses, her demands, she made everything new. Made him want. Made him greedy.

Because the one thing he hadn't expected was laughter.

This joy in his chest every time he watched her. The overwhelming urge to make this moment last forever.

* * *

Sam thought she might be floating on clouds. Or was it

that her body had never felt more like an instrument of pleasure?

Alessandro's weight on top of her as they sank into the bed…was heaven. The kiss he took while his chest crushed her breasts and his thick shaft perfectly notched up against her bare core left her reeling.

This kiss was a taking. A claiming, even. He didn't explore or tease or play, he simply ravished her mouth with a hunger that told her how long he'd wanted to do that.

Even better than the possessiveness of his kiss was the abandon with which she could touch him. The corded muscles of his neck, the hard slopes of his shoulder, the sparse hair on his defined chest, the ridges of his abdomen… In that moment, this powerful man was fully hers, and it went straight to her head. Eager for more, she thrust up her hips to dislodge him.

Instantly, he lifted his weight off her, his eyes frantically searching hers.

Fighting a smile, she snuck her hands lower, until she could cup his hard length. He was like warm steel through his trousers.

A soft gasp escaped her as she imagined him inside her, pounding away at her and, best of all, losing control as he chased his own climax.

"Please, I want to touch you."

Something danced in his eyes before he nodded.

Somehow, she managed to undo his trousers and snuck her hand inside. He was hard and hot and…big enough to startle her a little.

"*Cristo, bella,*" he whispered, his mouth buried in her temple.

Staring up at his stark features, she squeezed him and

stroked him from root to tip. The bead of pre-cum made her mouth water.

Head thrown back, Alessandro let out a grunt and a filthy curse that pinged against her skin. She did it a few more times, fascinated by the naked yearning in his face, before he arrested her wrist. "It's been a long while, Sameera. I would rather be inside you."

Sam bit her lip. "Has it been a long while out of choice?"

Slowly, he took her hand in his and laced their fingers. Then he moved off her, leaning on his side. They were both half-naked, and it was how he hesitated that made it so heart-wrenchingly intimate. She scooted closer, knowing the pull between their bodies was the anchor right then.

"I discovered, at a crisis point in my life, that I have an addictive nature." His gaze drifted away from the present. "It was either meaningless sex with strangers or… nothing. After I drowned myself in the first for a little while, I got disgusted with myself and stopped completely."

She traced the small scar through his brow. "I'm sorry it had to come to that."

He shrugged and kissed the back of her hand.

"Should I feel extra special, then?" she said, wriggling her brows in an exaggerated manner. Anything to chase away the dark shadows in his eyes.

Matteo had mentioned in an offhand comment once that his brother had lost the woman he had loved a long time ago. Now, all the pieces she knew about him began to form a picture that made her both like him and want to run away as far as possible.

His fingers sifted through her hair while a small smile played at his lips. The pad of his thumb traced her cheek with a reverence that filled her heart. "You're beautiful and witty and spirited. And probably a witch."

Pushing up, she kissed the corner of his mouth. Which he took full advantage of by devouring her mouth, again.

She was panting when she fell back against the bed, her fingers drawing doodles on his chest. The urgency to feel him inside her thrummed but this…this felt even more precious, more real. "I have to make this all very clinical by mentioning boring stuff. So much for a sophisticated summer fling."

He stilled, then nodded.

"I have an IUD." She cleared her throat. "Getting pregnant is dangerous for my heart condition. But when it's peak fertility time, I like to double up, just—"

"We'll use a condom."

Sam buried her face in his chest. "It's silly but—"

"Nothing about your health or your choices or your sense of safety is silly, *bella*. You insult me by suggesting otherwise."

Snuggling closer, she licked the line of his throat. "Thank you."

His fingers wrapped around her nape, before sliding into her hair, tugging her head up.

Smiling, he pressed a kiss to her temple. A hesitation danced in his eyes.

"Ask me whatever you want, Alessandro." She swallowed against that surge of affection she felt for him.

His fingers sifted through her hair slowly as he said, "You aren't resentful of the options that have been taken away from you?"

"Like babies? Or a long-term relationship with someone who might want the guarantee of a happy future?" she said, without missing a beat. "No."

She took a long breath, loving the intimacy of the dark night cloaking them like this. Loving that he was curious enough to want to know things about her. If this was just a fling, what would a real relationship with this man be like? "For a long time, all I wanted was to leave the hospital. Then it was being alone for an hour or two without my mom flipping out. Then came a solo shopping trip, an outing with friends, building to this confidence to go on a trip by myself. To tangle with an Italian stud. Now it's college and a career as an artist and traveling the world at some point." Looking at his stark, gorgeous features filled her with that joy of simply being there, in the moment with him. "I have so much to live for," she said, kissing the bristly underside of his jaw, "and I refuse to spend even a minute mourning the few things I can't have."

Nodding, he dipped his head, and this was a different kiss. It was soft and reverent and so full of promise that Sam couldn't sift through all the feelings it evoked.

The jarring tone of his cell phone broke the spell.

She straightened her dress as Alessandro answered his phone. A volley of Italian followed, bringing an instant pall over his features. Then he pressed a hand to his neck, a gesture that betrayed his discomfiture. "I have to go."

Sam looked out the large windows, out into the dark night beyond. "Now?"

"Sì."

Frowning, Sam got off the bed and followed him into

his cavernous closet. Even the sight of her clothes neatly hanging by his didn't throw her anymore.

"I have to go to Florence," he said softly, throwing a change of clothes into a small bag.

"Are you running away from me?" she whispered, giving voice to the crows pecking at her. In the flash of a second, it was as if the intimate world between them had fractured, thrusting him back into a reality she couldn't join.

He stilled. "I'm not a coward, *bella*."

"No, but you do like to control yourself, Alessandro." A long breath shuddered out of her as she claimed her power herself. "And I have challenged it from day one, no?"

Dropping the bag, he covered the distance between them to clasp her cheeks. "I have to visit a friend, an old woman in distress. And I can't abandon that responsibility because I'm desperate to fuck you." He pressed a quick kiss to her temple, then grabbed the bag. "If I get inside you, I won't want to leave."

Hurt found a tender spot in her. But she had power too in this relationship, whatever else he called it. She couldn't forget that.

"Are you saying that for my benefit or yours, Alessandro?"

Shock danced in his eyes before he left the bedroom, leaving her alone again.

CHAPTER NINE

SAM STEPPED OUT of the small, stuffy examination room and into the bright July afternoon. She smiled wide, loving the sunshine on her face. The cardiologist's office was located in a colorful piazza in the city of Como, a myriad of its intriguing lanes leading to grand galleries and beautiful churches.

Hitching her crossbody bag over her shoulder, she crossed the side street into the main thoroughfare and stilled.

Alessandro stood across the street, in his usual white dress shirt and dark trousers, leaning against a tinted Maserati and looking at his phone.

Even from the distance, the force of his presence hit her straight. Had he come to see her straight from the airport?

It had been two days since he'd left in the middle of the night. The next morning, Antonio had informed her that he'd gone straight to Tokyo.

He didn't owe her anything, she reminded herself again.

There was no future for them.

And yet, her belly knotted painfully every time she thought of returning home, of never being regarded again with that intense gaze, of never touching him again.

As if he felt her gaze on him, Alessandro looked up. Heat arched between them like a live wire. Her heart kicked against her rib cage. If it weren't for the fact that the cardiologist had told her she was perfectly fine, she'd have gone back in.

He crossed the street in long strides. But he didn't haul her into his arms or kiss her cheek or even pat her shoulder, as horrifically platonic as that sounded. In fact, he left at least a foot between them. Something told Sam it was a conscious decision, to stop himself. And just like that, her entire mood took a downswing.

She couldn't believe it was the same man who had gone down on her as if she were a feast he was starved for.

"What's wrong?" he had the gall to ask.

"Nothing. When did you get back?"

He jerked his chin at the building behind her. "How did your appointment go?"

"How did you know I'd be here?" she countered.

"Your phone was off, and no one at the villa knew where you were." An edge crept into his words. "Angelina told me."

"It's on Airplane mode. The roaming charges will be astronomical," she said, waving her phone. "I don't want to send my parents into debt again. When I'm at the villa, I connect to Wi-Fi." She sensed his hesitation—no, frustration. How were they starting off on such a wrong note? "Don't freeze me out. Just say what you want to."

"I have a phone and a chauffeured car I want you to use."

"Isn't that overkill?"

"I would like to reach you when I want to, Sameera."

"You say my name like that when you're railroading me into something."

He rubbed his brow with his fingertip, a sure tell that he was employing about hundred filters between his real feelings and what he said. "Is it such a pain to accommodate me?"

Was she imagining the flash of vulnerability in his eyes?

Sam sighed. It wasn't as if she wasn't eating his food, staying at his house, sleeping in his damned bed already. "Okay."

His jaw relaxed. "What did they say?"

"Just a routine checkup."

He ran the pad of his thumb under her eyes. Sam wanted to lean into the touch so badly that she swayed. "You look tired, *bella*."

"Is that all you see when you see me, Alessandro? Someone you have to check up on?"

He flinched at her sharp tone. And that made her feel like gum stuck on her shoe.

Hands tucked into his trousers, he watched her. "I can't seem to stop upsetting you." Hardness crawled into his words, etched into his features. "As long as you're mine, I'll worry over you, Sameera. I will not apologize for being the way I am."

Her mouth fell open. "Is that how you see me? As… yours?"

He frowned as if she was being dense on purpose. *"Sì."*

She should address the deeper issue here, but all she felt was this fizzy feeling, as if she were filled with bubbles of joy. Was this about seeing her as someone who was incapable, or about his needing to be in control?

"I haven't been sleeping well because I've been painting. What I had in mind, it's taking shape on the canvas." *He* was taking shape on her canvas, and she couldn't stop obsessing over it. "I'm at that stage where I just want to keep going, night or day. I don't care about sleep or food—"

Her stomach interrupted them with an embarrassingly loud growl. She'd slept in late and had to rush to the appointment. Which meant she'd missed breakfast. In the scheme of things, it wasn't a big thing. Until her body decided to turn it into a big thing.

Her own stubbornness kept her from admitting she was wrong. "Why aren't you at work?"

"Day off."

"Oh." In the weeks she'd been at the villa, she'd heard Maria complain that Alessandro worked ninety-hour weeks without a break. Even Antonio had asked his son to take it easy. "What were you planning to do?"

"Go to bed and stay there all day. With you."

All the doubts died an instant death, and Sam threw herself at him.

Wrapping her fingers around his neck, she pressed her mouth to his. Despite everything, all she wanted was to kiss him.

She tasted his surprise in his stillness. His mouth was soft and tasted of coffee, and he was hard and warm against her body. When she moaned in complaint, he laughed and opened for her. She licked into his mouth eagerly.

But he didn't deepen the kiss.

Instead, his mouth was soft, exploring, almost…reverent. His emotions buffeted her, carrying her along. This kiss wasn't like the one in his study. Or the one in the kitchen. This wasn't a prelude to sex. No rushing toward a destination. This kiss said he wanted nothing more than to be here with her in this moment.

She buried her face in his chest, loving the thunder of his heart against her cheek. Part of her didn't want to keep acknowledging what he was becoming to her. But part of her knew this moment would be over soon.

Some of the tension she'd felt in his frame dissipated. That he liked her telling him how he made her feel was obvious. Why didn't he reciprocate?

No, she wasn't going to analyze this. He'd taken the day off to spend it with her. That said more than words ever could. "By the way, I'm very competitive when it comes to these things."

He tucked a lock of her hair behind her ear, and she buried a smile that wanted to bloom. "What things?"

Casually, she took his hand and laced his fingers with hers. That infinitesimal stillness came over him, but he shook it off. She dragged him toward the noisy piazza. "Two-point-five to nothing. I want to even that score."

"Two-point-five?"

"Our orgasm count."

His laughter exploded onto the quiet street. The sound dug its very roots into her heart. More than one woman stopped and stared at the stunning picture he made.

Her fingers tightened around his—something dark and possessive blooming in her chest. She wanted to drag him back to the privacy of their bedroom, to cup that laughter and hide it away for herself. She wanted the other women to stop looking at him. "Alessandro?"

"Si?"

"I know you said this is a fling, but I'm out if you…

if you even look at someone else." She sounded particularly bloodthirsty, but she didn't care.

"Okay." His gray eyes were warm when he looked down at her. "How did you come up with the half?"

Sam pushed the stubborn lock of hair from his forehead back. "The half comes from me trying to…" she licked her lips "…to get off to you the other night after you left. I didn't quite manage it."

Naked desire made his eyes pop. "Then, let's go. I want to see how well you keep all these promises."

"I've got another appointment." Something darkened in his gaze, and she hurried to explain. "With Giuseppe, this guy I met at the club."

"The exclusive thing works both ways, Sameera." Pure steel in his tone.

They started walking again. Instantly, he adjusted his pace to match hers. "He's a painter," Sam said.

"What do you know about him?"

"Angelina's already checked him out. She's as overbearing as you."

"Now I know why I always liked her."

Sam laughed at his sarcasm. "I can't ditch Giuseppe. It's a series of…appointments."

"Sounds important."

"He's painting me. Nude."

Alessandro stopped walking. "Going all in on this vacation, *bella*?"

Sam nodded.

He rubbed his neck. "What made you decide to do this all of a sudden?"

"Well, you saw the dress I wore to the club. I met

Giuseppe there, and we got to talking about different painting techniques. At first, he—"

"Asked you to go home with him," Alessandro supplied.

"I said I wasn't interested. He said it was bad luck for him. We chatted a bit, then he asked me about the scar. He said he'd love to paint me nude for a series he's doing about imperfect bodies. Usually, I wouldn't have agreed. But it took me a long time to have a healthy relationship with my body. This is a way of celebrating it."

"You should," Alessandro said softly.

"Is it weird that I wish you were a little jealous that another man will see me naked?"

"Oh, I am, *tesoro*. But—"

"We aren't in a real relationship. I know," Sam said before he could.

"I was going to say that's my problem to deal with. Not yours."

"Oh."

"Is he going to sell it?"

"Of course. I wish I could buy it myself. But I've seen his work, and I can't afford it." It had made her feel strange at first, the idea that someone would own a nude painting of her. But she also wanted her body, her courage in this small act, to be a source of inspiration and joy for another. "He's offering me a chunky model's fee, though. It will be displayed at a gallery in a few months. The tickets are already sold out."

Sam eyed the peaceful square. The sunny day, the colorful shops and restaurants and Alessandro's fingers clasped around her, it was a moment out of her dreams.

She wanted the dark intimacy of his desire, but she

wanted this time with him even more. She wanted to talk to him, get to know him. She wanted to steal away pieces of him whether he was willing to part with them or not.

"I have a couple of hours before the sitting," she said, managing to sound breezy. "Keep me company until then?"

"If you promise to go to bed on time tonight," he countered instantly.

"Fine." She dragged him to a faded but cheerful yellow table away from the rest, one with a chess board drawn into its worn grain.

When she went for the chair opposite him, he tugged her into his lap. And then he took her mouth with a roughness that made her gasp. On and on the kiss went, his tongue thrusting in an erotic dance that made her cheeks heat.

A little urgency, a lot of impatience and a whole lot of darkly possessive declaration that she was his—despite who saw her naked—the kiss was eloquent.

"Whether I sleep or not is up to you, isn't it?" she whispered, when he released her. "I'm not letting you leave me alone in that bed again."

That raised brow greeted her like an old friend.

It was the warmth he got in his eyes when she argued with him, the hitch of his mouth when he smiled at her, that little tic in his jaw when his control was teetering on the edge that returned that fizzy feeling to her chest.

Alessandro knew he should've waited for her at the villa, waited for her to finish her appointments and come to him. He could catch up on much-needed sleep, try to recoup the time he'd lost because he'd walked away from two more days of business meetings.

But he was done denying himself this small pocket of pleasure.

To leave Sam that night, her soft pliant body, her flushed face, her wide smile had been the hardest thing he'd ever had to do.

Not just because what he wanted was to be buried inside her, because he wanted to discover if having Sam, if losing himself in her body, would rid him of this… obsession. This constant need. This…voracious hunger.

She looked like a sunflower when she teased him. Or laughed with him. Or when she mentioned orgasms and blushed fiercely. Or when she got mad at him. Or when she tried to hide how much he hurt her or how aroused she got around him.

Every minute with her was like standing alone in an entire field of sunflowers. He constantly felt as if he'd miss something precious or that he could spend a lifetime with her and still be unable to take it all in.

The want she made him feel was a drive for life. A fire in his belly. A newfound appreciation for each day, each minute. As if she were introducing him back to himself, one facet at a time. And he was on constant edge, trying to manage it all. Trying to not feel so much. Trying to do damage control for when she left him and suddenly he had no one but himself again. Nothing but a yawning ocean of loneliness in front of him.

The alternative that he could ask her to stay was unthinkable. Unbearable.

"What are your plans for fall?" he said, once their orders were out of the way.

"Starting college for a business degree. Eventually, I want to stretch beyond just oil paintings. They're tedious and time-consuming, but I love them. I need to build passive income streams." She dipped her fork into the pasta and took a big bite. "It would be fun if I can get out of California, but out of state means I'll end up with huge loans. Also, I don't think Mom can take it. A community college is my best bet."

"If you need money for college, I'll pay..." He cleared his throat when she pinned him with a fierce look. "I will loan it to you."

She cast him a sweet look that packed a punch. If he weren't so damned turned on by her temper, by her clever moves in chess, by her voracious appetite, that sweet sarcasm that made her eyes pop would've floored him. "And why would you do that?"

"Because I have more money than I know what to do with, *tesoro*." Irritation coated his words. How did he explain to her that he wanted to remain a part of her life even when he wasn't there? He didn't understand it himself. "Like I said, it can be a loan." There, he was even making all kinds of adjustments for her.

"So we're going to keep in touch after I leave?"

He suppressed the fingers of panic that rose at that idea. "You're being difficult on purpose."

"Just establishing the etiquette for after-fling behavior."

"Sameera..."

"It's bad enough I haven't told Mom everything. The last thing I want to explain to her is where I got the college tuition from."

"You haven't told her—"

"That I've swapped brothers? No."

"Don't say it like that."

"That's what everyone thinks. Even Angelina. Though, she won't say it to my face." She ran the tip of his finger down his tight jaw. "It doesn't bother me."

It bothered him. Not what people thought of him and her, but how they treated her, how they saw her. That his brother would always have a claim on her affection bothered him.

It was the height of hypocrisy after he'd declared that this was nothing but a fling. But he wanted no other man to have such significance in her life. No other man to know her as well as he did.

Cristo, there was nothing rational in this.

"Mom will say you're taking advantage of me," she said, that familiar rancor back in her voice. "At least your aunt puts the blame at my feet."

"*Zia* knows? How's that a good thing that she blames you?"

"Because she thinks I have enough sense to make my own decisions. Even if they're morally wrong. As to why..." she bit her lip "...Matteo told your parents. He's continuing his I-will-admit-all-my-sins phase."

"And as usual, he doesn't think of anyone else. Was *Zia*...rude to you?"

Her smile made him relax. "Oh, she's far too nice to say anything to my face, Alessandro. You know that. But she's been considerably cooler toward me. I caught something in Italian along the lines of...*coming between brothers*, but who knows? To give him credit, Matteo did explain that he'd cheated on me. Clearly that doesn't absolve me of the sin of trapping you when I was done with him."

"You didn't trap me, *bella*. If anything—"

"What, Alessandro? You trapped my poor, naïve, unsophisticated self, is that it? Seduced me away from your brother because I didn't know better?"

He realized then that he could hurt her, in ways he hadn't understood until then. Gripping her chin, he tugged until she looked into his eyes. "Thinking like that means invalidating everything you've endured, everything that makes you who you are today. I'll never again make the mistake of thinking you less than who you are, *tesoro*. All of you."

Shock flared her eyes wide. Swallowing, she looked away from him.

How did he tell her it wasn't their age difference or her health or Matteo that bothered him? That it was his lack of control when it came to her, his ever-growing need to steal her away from the world, to protect her, even from himself, that ate through him?

It didn't matter that this was temporary. That she thought of this as an adventure, that she probably even considered him to be a dangerous, exotic once-in-a-lifetime ride she'd never try again.

Christo, even that didn't dent his self-esteem. On the contrary, he found immense pleasure in the fact that she found him attractive, more so than his own brother.

Whatever he told himself, it didn't change the intensity of his feelings for her. Didn't change the fact that he was beginning to crave more and more of her, even knowing there was no future for them.

Before the moment could be fractured by his incapability to verbalize his chaotic thoughts, his chauffeur appeared at their table with a bag in his hand. He took the bag and handed it to Sameera.

She tore through the packaging and spread the contents out onto the table in front of him. Little jars of oil paints in a rainbow of colors and a variety of brushes and a bunch of other things he'd picked cluttered the table, tinkling against each other. If it were up to him, he'd have bought the entire store.

"There's more," he added, his heart crawling into his throat at her stunned expression.

His first impulse had been to buy her jewelry. He'd discarded the idea immediately. He wanted her to remember him when she left.

Now every time she painted using one of these colors, she'd think of him.

Really, he was a selfish bastard.

Her fingers shook as she picked a glass jar with amber color that glittered in the sunlight. "These brushes and paints...they're super expensive. How did you even know this brand was the..." Then she gasped, eyes going impossibly wide in her small face.

Unable to help himself, he ran his knuckles over the sharp jut of her collarbones, once again marveling at the dizzying complexity of how fragile she looked and how strong she was beneath. And while she'd bash him on the head if he told her, both parts enthralled him.

The strength and the fragility...everything about her called to him.

"It's the best gift anyone's ever given me."

And then she was back in his lap, trailing kisses all over his face, whispering things he couldn't make out, and he thought it was the happiest he'd ever been.

CHAPTER TEN

Sam woke up to find the bedroom bathed in strips of moonlight.

Alessandro had picked her up outside Giuseppe's apartment, having waited for two hours. She'd fallen asleep the moment he'd started the car. By the time she'd showered, he had disappeared.

Blinking, she sat up and found him in the armchair. Legs kicked out in front, fingers clasped on his abdomen, eyes closed. His dark hair gleamed with wetness, that aura of quiet confidence clinging to him in repose too.

Gray sweatpants hung low on his hips, and his bare chest was lean but defined.

She moved to stand in front of him, skin thrumming with molten awareness. For all that he claimed that this was an affair, they still hadn't had sex. If anything, he seemed almost…reluctant. All her insecurities about how inexperienced she was crashed into her.

With Matteo, sex had been another milestone, a rite of passage, even another item in her adulting checklist. She had wanted the experience more than she had wanted him specifically, which was horrible and stupid in hindsight.

With Alessandro, though, all she wanted was to lose herself in him and make him lose all sense of control.

"Sameera?" he said, coming awake. "Everything okay?"

"Why didn't you join me in bed?"

He straightened in the armchair, the soft light from the standing lamp making his pecs shine. "You didn't invite me in."

"What do you think the last few weeks have been about?" she snarled, throat tight.

"You were deeply asleep," he said in that same calm tone. "I didn't want to disturb you."

"You want me or not?"

He spread his legs in a wicked invitation, and her gaze slid down his body. The shape of his long, thick erection, evident against his sweatpants, made her skin prickle. His gray gaze patiently waited for her to come back. "I'm always like this now, *tesoro*. All it takes is a thought of you."

Squaring her shoulders, she moved forward until she was straddling his legs. Putting her weight on the armrest, she climbed into his lap. His thighs were rock hard against her flesh, and his scent of cloves and pine wrapped around her like a tendril of lust.

His palms stroked her hips, her ass, her thighs, over and over. The scrape of his abrasive palms against her smooth skin left pockets of heat behind. Those gray eyes searched hers. "You're nervous, *bella*." His hands drifted upward, spanning the tight curve of her waist, rough knuckles brushing the underside of her breasts but not lingering. "We'll take it slow, Sameera," he said, a ragged edge to his words. His open mouth drew a wet-hot trail over her jaw.

Swatting his hands away, Sam scooted upward on his thighs until his cock speared her, notching perfectly against her clit. "I don't want slow or controlled, Alessandro. I want to consume you, break you apart. Until I know you like no one else does."

Squeezing her hips hard, he jostled her on his throbbing length, just enough to send dampness pooling at her core. "Why, *bella*?"

Leaning down, she bit his lower lip. "I don't know, okay? I…have never felt like this before."

"In that, we are not apart, *tesoro*." Then took her mouth in their hottest, hungriest kiss yet.

Sam couldn't catch her breath. She didn't want to. He ravaged her mouth, breathing out endearments when she willingly took it and curses when she got aggressive. His tongue thrust into her mouth in a vulgar parody of what she needed somewhere else. He whispered things in Italian she didn't understand but made her shiver.

He stroked and kneaded every rise and dip of her curves. His fingers moved up and down, charting her skin. On every downward slide, they pressed against her breasts, but never touching enough, never following through.

"Please, Alessandro, just come inside me now…"

"No, *bella*. Let's get you ready first, or I will hurt you."

Sam moaned into his mouth, desperate for him to be as mindless as her. "I want fast and furious," she said biting at his lower lip.

He shook his head, his hands busy rolling up the hem of her T-shirt. "Not for our first time, no."

She lost her protest as her shirt came off. Long fingers circled her nipples, which were tight and achy even without touch. His palm flat on her belly, he pushed her until she was leaning back, her hair a silky waterfall down her bare back.

Her balance as precarious as her heart's yearning, Sam bowed back.

Something dark and wicked shone in his eyes as they trailed over her breasts and lower. Much lower where her pink thong was mostly damp and swallowed up by her folds. "You're so beautiful, Sam. I don't know where to begin. If I'm not careful, I could—"

"I don't want careful, Alessandro," Sam said, leaning forward. "If so, we should stop now before I—"

Another kiss and this one was pure male dominance, with all his expertise pitted against her relative inexperience.

His fingers trailed all over again, tracing her scar, playing with her breasts, drawing circles around her nipples, tugging at the diamond piercing at her belly button, leaving pockets of heat wherever they went.

"God, you're such a tease." Sinking her fingers into his hair, she tugged.

Laughing against her thudding heart, he bent. Tongued her nipple in a wet lash. Did it over and over, a featherlight touch that disappeared too fast for her to pin down.

She looked down, and he looked up as his mouth closed over the taut peak. That simple, searing eye contact was the most erotic thing she'd ever known.

How Alessandro looked at her—as if everything about her was fascinating, as if he couldn't get enough—was just as arousing as what he did to her with that mouth. He thrummed her other nipple with his fingers as he drew the first one into his mouth and suckled, hard.

Rivulets of sensation zoomed down to concentrate at her core.

Fighting his hold, she moved up on him, and they both groaned. He sucked and tugged at her nipples until she was so sensitive that she couldn't take it anymore. She writhed on him, trying to find the right angle, while release hovered just out of reach.

Sinking her fingers into his hair, she tugged hard. "Give me what I need. Make me come. Now."

"I told you I like you best demanding and clingy." With that, he ripped her thong off. His thumb found her clit and stroked, slower and gentler than she needed, fingers dipping into her wetness.

"*Cristo*, you're so wet," he said and then dripped her dampness all over her clit. Over and over, up and down, he played with her folds, flicked her clit but not enough to get her off.

Sam bent her spine, buried her mouth in his neck and bit him.

His laughter joined the symphony of sensations sizzling across her skin, a kaleidoscope of pleasure urging her on and on. Then slowly, ever so gently, he penetrated her. One finger, then two.

The fit was tight and burned, and Sam never wanted him to stop.

"*Maledizione*, you clench me so tightly. What will you do to my cock, Sameera?" He thrust his fingers in and out, stretching her, his long fingers pressing and nudging a spot inside of her that made her shudder.

Sam rocked in tune with his thrusts, every inch of her coalescing at that spot.

On and on, he caressed her, urging her on with his

filthy words. Never shifting his gaze from hers. She was chasing his mouth at her nipples for a deeper pull, his fingers inside her for a better angle, but it was his eyes that made her fly.

One second it wasn't enough and the next too much. Pleasure fluttered its wings across her body, spiraling down and down, until it splintered. She moaned and rocked into it, desperate to hold on.

Alessandro lavished openmouthed kisses over her neck and shoulders, his fingers still wrenching the aftertremors inside her.

"You come so prettily, Sam. The sounds you make..." he said, his mouth at her temple, his fingers pulling out of her with a squishy sound, leaving her feeling achingly empty. "I need to feel you bare, *bella*."

Then he was pushing down his sweatpants onto his corded thighs, pulling her up onto his abdomen until his shaft pressed up against her sensitized clit. The heat from his skin burned her, the slide of that thick length against her folds making her arch into him.

"Inside me," Sam whispered. As long as he made her feel like this again. As long as he looked at her as if he wanted to consume her. "Now, Alessandro."

She was a rag doll in his arms as he lifted her up, tore open a condom packet and rolled it down his length. And then the broad head of his erection notched at her entrance. The sight of him playing with her folds, draping himself in her wetness...made new embers heat through her.

Sam watched in growing fascination and spiraling alarm. He was big, and it had been so long for her. It was going to hurt. Just as she braced herself to not betray too much, he cupped her hips, lifting her.

Panting, she pushed down her weight, hands on the slopes of his shoulders. "No, here. Now."

"Even if you've come, it will hurt like this. You're fragile." His refusal was steel even as his gray gaze was hazy with lust.

It was the wrong word to use on her. She wanted no accommodation, no second-guessing on his part. She wanted him to take her without apologies.

She went for his mouth. She licked and laved at his lips, nipped and bit, stroked her tongue against his until his hands wandered away from her hips to cup her breasts. He cupped and played with them, the tips of his fingers flicking against her nipples.

He groaned as she pushed up to her knees, took him in her hand and dipped the head of his shaft inside. One inch, then two. She hissed as even that stretched her impossibly. The burn of it made his kiss that much keener, sweeter.

With one downward thrust, she impaled herself on him. His hips thrust up instinctively, as though he couldn't stop himself. Which meant he stroked into her fluttering channel in one hard thrust, until he was lodged all the way in.

His palm on her shoulder held her down from jerking away. He went so deep that Sam wondered if he'd ever not been a part of her.

The pain came then. A flash of sharp, achy burn that meant she couldn't keep from crying out. His long, filthy curse accompanied it. Sam breathed in a long gulp and breathed out.

Fingers gripped her chin roughly, tilting her head down. His eyes were stormy, the black at the center swallowing up the gray like a dark cloud. "You're the most infuriating, outrageous—"

Sam stole another kiss. She wasn't experienced enough to seduce him—not yet, but she knew him now. Knew what he liked. Knew he wanted her more than he let on. Knew to tease him and taunt him until his control shattered.

So she swallowed his anger. Cajoled with her mouth. Petted him with everything she had in her. Begged him. Told him how much she wanted him to move inside her. How she'd struggled to shed her inhibitions before. How she wanted no one but him.

He pulled away with a harsh exhale, brows tied. "You're not naïve at all, *tesoro*. You're conniving and manipulative, and I could have really hurt you."

Sam nipped his lower lip, the harsh edge of his voice curling around her spine. "What I am is determined, Alessandro, to have you. In every way possible."

The fire in his eyes refused to thaw. "You should've let me take you slowly—"

She caught his upper lip with her teeth this time, and he groaned and took over the kiss. For a few seconds, there was nothing but the sounds of their mouths tugging and licking.

A fervent urgency filled her, and she trailed her mouth down his jaw to that hollow in his neck that called to her. She licked him, tasting the salt and sweat of his skin, breathed him in, and still it wasn't enough.

It amazed her that she could touch him like this, warm muscle and sinew and skin. She wished she could touch his heart too. Wished she could write her name on it, like a name tag to claim possession.

"Do you know you say a lot of *you should*s to me? Also, every time you say Sameera in that forbidding tone, it makes me want to defy you, just on principle."

His hands, finally, moved from where they'd had clamped around her hips to stop her from moving. Mouth buried in her neck, he touched her breasts, pinched her nipples and dragged his hands down to play with her clit until she was dripping again and the intrusion of him burned less.

"I promised myself that I would never hurt you, Sam."

"And I told you to not treat me as if I were fragile, Alessandro. This momentary pain, which is already gone by the way, is nothing for me."

Sam shifted her hips experimentally. Jesus, it felt good. More than good. It felt amazing. So she did it again, and his answering thrust came a breath later. Their groans rippled through the air around them. Her channel still felt unbearable achy and full, but that only amplified every little twang of pleasure.

Before she could build a rhythm, he pushed up to his feet, and the movement sent sensation rippling where they were joined.

Her back hit his bed, a cool embrace in contrast to the wall of warmth at her front. She grimaced when he slipped out of her.

Climbing up after her, he didn't miss it. The night lamp she'd turned on bathed his naked body in strips of light. Straddling her, he bent down and kissed her. "Shall I take what I want, then, Sameera?"

"Yes. It's all I want. If you hurt me, you'll make it

better. Don't you get what this is all about, Alessandro? I trust you. I want you. I'm here with you because you make me want to take risk after risk."

His forehead pressed to hers, he drew in a sharp, shuddering breath.

He said nothing with his mouth after that. Oh, but his lips, and kisses and nips and licks and hands and caresses and grunts said everything…

He built her up all the way to the edge before he thrust into her. Except for a pinch that lasted a few seconds, it was that achy, stretching fullness when he was inside her. Even then, he gave her time to get used to him.

Kissed her, licked her, laved her…and then he picked up his pace as he angled her body the way he wanted it, pushing her knee into her chest. Every thrust hit a spot inside of Sam that seemed to hold it all tightly together.

And then there were his fingers at her clit, and his thrusts hit that spot again and again, and she was nothing but spiraling sensation, and on the next breath she exploded into a million fragments and screamed his name and clung to him, and he shifted her again and then he was pounding into her, hard enough to make her see stars, hard enough for her core to take a battering, hard enough for the heavy bed to creak and moan, and then he pinned her down with his hips, arresting her movements, using her body for nothing but his pleasure, and his release when it came made him shudder in her arms, and a roar fell from his mouth, and it was the sweetest sound Sam had ever heard.

Alessandro watched as Sameera slipped into a deep sleep, one arm thrown around him, feet tucked in between his own. His heart beat like it was on steroids, even though his release had been hours ago.

She had been sore after but wouldn't admit to it when he'd carried her into the shower. Had seen the marks he'd left on her skin and liked them. Had understood finally how much she trusted him.

And yet, that trust didn't feel like a weight, like his other relationships. Her expectations that he take everything he wanted from her was like undoing a shackle he'd wound around himself.

She asked for nothing and yet somehow took everything he had.

It felt like discovering a patch of sunlight after living in shadows and darkness. Like a gift he wasn't sure he deserved.

As dawn's pink and orange light illuminated the room, he gathered her closer. Marveled at how easily he could get used to sleeping with her wrapped around him like this. To wake up with her like this for a million mornings.

Sated in body and mind, he couldn't stop his heart from wondering about the shape of a future with her.

CHAPTER ELEVEN

ALESSANDRO DIDN'T GO into work for two whole weeks. The day after the weekend, his cell phone blew up enough for Sam to know how unprecedented it was.

The first three or four days, she ate and slept and woke to have sex. For his part, he fed her in bed, drew her rose-scented baths, cajoled her into a game of chess and, when she was in that sleepy, lazy state, played the piano for hours. Only coming to bed when she dragged him to it, pulling at his stiff fingers.

He was insatiable. She was even more so. For years, she'd wondered if sex would ever be something she craved. If her history had somehow inhibited her ability to simply let go, to live in the moment. She definitely had frustrated Matteo on more than one occasion with her lukewarm responses and halfhearted interest.

But now, she knew the taste of that mindless craving.

Alessandro and his kisses, caresses, lazy lovemaking and sudden bouts of have-to-be-inside-you put paid to any and all doubts she'd ever harbored.

On day four, they ventured into his study through the secret corridor to pick up something to read. Because her body needed a break and he needed a distraction, he'd declared.

She'd discovered she had muscles in places she hadn't even given a thought to. They'd spent hours lazing in separate recliners, discussing Jane Austen and classical music. Then they played chess while eating cheese and fruit.

On the way back, she'd kissed him in the darkness, feeling that urgency of having wasted too many precious hours. That itch beneath the skin that wanted to touch him, lose herself in him. He'd offered token protest, groaned when she'd bit him, picked her up, propped her up against the wall as if she weighed nothing and then thrust into her.

She had been ready. He'd checked. Still, the first thrust had felt raw and rough and painful but oh so glorious. When she'd been unable to hide her grimace on the second thrust, he'd pulled out, sunk to his knees, whispered apologies and soft kisses into her belly and then made her come again with the featherlight flicks of his tongue.

She'd been sobbing at the end, alternately begging for more and for him to stop.

By the time the next weekend rolled around, he'd thoroughly trounced her at chess, in so few moves that all her competitiveness spilled out. When she had attacked him on the bed, outraged that he'd pretended to lose to her until now, he'd let her straddle him and then, while he was inside her, he'd confided that she'd beaten him the other times because he'd been far too distracted imagining her in all kinds of positions.

On the eighth day, he worked from home while she painted in the studio he'd arranged for her. Tongue in cheek, she had said she could bear it if he went in to

Milan for work, but he'd insisted on staying near her. He'd ruined her concentration by coming to his knees in front of her, punishing—or rewarding—her for teasing him.

They were both people used to silence, who craved solitude and yet somehow to find it with each other too. As if their silences had their own language to communicate with. They spent hours together not talking, her painting, him working, then coming together in a flash of biting kisses and rough, needy sex.

Sam didn't understand the magic of their togetherness and decided against trying.

As remote and untouchable he was, Alessandro said hello when she called her cousin Kavi who never coddled or was condescending to her. He'd been shirtless and looked thoroughly debauched, and when Sam had ambushed him because Kavi begged to see *who Sam was tapping*, he played along with his arms wrapped around her while Kavi gushed over his good looks and teased Sam with horribly intrusive questions. Alessandro had then informed Kavi in that deep voice that Sam had seduced him with her stubbornness... It was the moment Sam knew he had her heart. Faulty and courageous as it was, it had gone over into his keeping.

And she also knew the inevitability of it shattering into so many pieces soon and of being able to do nothing to stop it.

They were like a newly married couple on their honeymoon, Angelina told a stunned Sam when she'd come down for breakfast on the second weekend. Sam hadn't been expecting all of the Riccis to be right there in the kitchen having breakfast.

Alessandro still worked from the villa, and Sam had started painting him with oils. They escaped one evening to a museum, which had of course been emptied of people for him. Because he didn't want the world to intrude on her time with the art, he'd said.

Dismayed, Sam stared down at her short shorts and old T-shirt of Alessandro's. It wasn't indecent, but it was an undisputed announcement to a kitchen and backyard full of family, cousins and close friends.

How was she to know that her sudden cravings for carbs would result in all of the Riccis bearing witness to her walk of shame? Was it a walk of shame if she wasn't ashamed of all the things she'd done with him?

Sam filled her coffee cup blushing beetroot red no doubt and said hello to people Maria insisted on introducing her to. Several male cousins winked at her. A couple of aunts looked her up and down, as if to see what all the fuss was about. One, introduced as Lucia, muttered something about violets.

Looking away, Sam took the picnic basket a beaming Maria handed her, piled with enough food to last them another week, and tried not to run. But even in her haste, she didn't miss the fact that Alessandro's aunt had loaded it up with protein bars, the kind she liked, and yogurt cups.

She'd almost teared up on the stairs. Yep, she'd finally reached the stage where her body had been through such a wringer that facing reality felt like a hard crash.

She had half finished a protein bar by the time she returned to his suite.

Alessandro was at the piano. Back bare, spine erect, sweatpants sitting low on his hips, playing another heart-wrenching tune.

Sam stood at the door and listened, loath to disturb him. Even to her untrained ears, it was clear that he was a gifted pianist. It was his one addiction he didn't smother. The music soared through her, filling her, saying things she knew Alessandro would never put into words.

She loved seeing him like this, knowing him in this moment. More intimate than sex. Knowing without doubt that no one else crossed the barrier he put between himself and the world. Not even his family.

And yet he had let her in.

Despite all his warnings, he'd opened himself to her. He'd made the last few weeks the best time of her life, even when they'd been fighting, even when he'd been rejecting this thing between them.

"Sam?" he said, turning around.

"FYI," she said, swinging the basket onto the coffee table, "not my fault if people ask you later about planning a wedding."

The shutter fell down so hard in his eyes that he might as well have slammed a door in her face. "Sameera…"

"It's a joke, Alessandro." Her laughter released with a hard edge she couldn't hide. "I wouldn't be able to tolerate your controlling personality beyond this tawdry affair."

Something tightened in his face, giving his features that saturnine cast. "I did not realize this was *tawdry* to you."

And she realized, with dawning dismay, that she had just hurt him. Worse, she had done it to see if she could.

"Okay, maybe *tawdry* isn't the word. But I definitely fit the label of a *mistress*. You have spent a fortune on just my painting supplies, and we rarely go anywhere."

"All you had to do was ask to go somewhere, *bella*. And you're not my mistress," he said, looking down his nose. As if the very word was offensive to his entire being. "What put you in such a mood?" he said, his anger already under control. As if she were still that puzzle.

Sam sighed. "Your entire family, extended included, is in the kitchen, overflowing into the patio." She tugged at the neckline of her T-shirt. "They're celebrating Matteo's progress to the wheelchair."

"He'll tire himself out."

"Angelina's watching him like a hawk." She gathered her tangled hair and redid her messy bun. "I wish I hadn't walked into the kitchen looking like this. Honestly," she said and something ugly and hot crawled into her throat and refused to dislodge, "I don't like attention, and I definitely don't like being looked at as though I—"

"How do you think you look, Sameera?"

"Disheveled. Like I just crawled out of bed after a week-long sex session. Like I'm not good enough for you."

"Maybe it's the other way around, *bella*. Maybe they think I'm too old, too jaded, too much of an arrogant asshole for someone like you. As for how you look…" his lashes fell and rose "…you're beautiful." It wasn't what he wanted to say. "As to my family, they have no boundaries."

She shrugged, that angry itchy feeling persisting under her skin. "If you want to join the party, please go ahead. I might catch a nap."

"Not interested."

"Won't they expect you?"

"Not even if I didn't have you here with me," he said, a small smile wreathing his lips. "I'm not into parties or crowds either. I don't go to clubs. I don't spend hours with friends. I'm...sort of a loner."

She nodded, struck again by how alike they were. "I met your great-aunt Lucia. It was interesting."

Sam was sure his aunt had said Sam could never be Violetta. And that was it—the source of her sudden, unnamed distress.

The woman had Alessandro had loved and lost. The one that Angelina had accidentally dropped into their conversations more than once. The one he clearly still loved after all these years. "I think she also mumbled *Indian*, *too thin*, *too American* and something else before she turned up her rather beaky nose at me. Apparently, no aspect of me lives up to her standards."

Violetta...the name pinged around in her brain, hitting the walls, out of control, the echoes increasing and spiraling and amplifying until it was all she heard. She even raised her hands to close them over her ears. As if she could shut it out.

And Sam knew, like she'd known that first moment when she'd seen him that something was changing within her, with that intuitive certainty, that Violetta had meant everything to him. That the Alessandro Sam had got was the after-Violetta version. That she'd only got a part of him, not the whole.

Loving Violetta and losing her had changed him. And suddenly, it felt unbearable that he still belonged to that ghost from the past. That he wasn't hers completely. Even the splintered version of his heart that was left wasn't hers.

He wasn't offering it to her.

But she wanted it.

"Aunt Lucia is an old crone who doesn't approve of anyone. She calls my cousin's wife a crow to her face."

"So the fact that I haven't been assigned a bird is a compliment?"

"You want compliments, Sam?" he said, spreading his legs as if to make space for her. "I will give them to you."

"Don't patronize me," she said, feeling wonky in her own skin. Even at her sickest, she'd never felt this disoriented. As if she was falling endlessly.

"You're upset." He frowned and swept his gaze all over her. "Come, Sameera," he said in that calm, quiet voice that sent shivers down her spine. "I will make you feel better, *bella*."

"I don't want what you're offering. Not today," she said, her own voice breathless and shallow.

He didn't call her out on her bad temper. Instead, he leaned his elbows against the piano, pushed his legs forward and waited. As if he were offering himself to her.

Afternoon sunlight poured through the window, over the olive-toned skin stretched taut over lean muscles. With that much light dappling over him, she could see the small imperfections that made him so gorgeous— the small scar under his chin, the slight bifurcation in his right brow, the too-tight jut of his cheekbones that gave him such a severe profile, the spot on his neck that he'd missed while shaving last night because she'd distracted him...

God, she was becoming dizzyingly addicted to running her fingers through the hair that coated his chest, the slight flare of his nostrils when he wanted to have sex and the predatory stillness that followed because his first instinct was to control the impulse, the warmth of his eyes that betrayed how much he liked her... She wished she could capture him with her brushes in this moment.

But more than that, she wanted to stay in this moment with him forever. And that was a terrifying thought that had been returning with an unerring frequency.

But right now, something else trumped fear. Right now, she felt bloodthirsty, possessive, feral in a way she'd been before. She wanted to claim him as hers.

The moment she reached him, his hands slipped under her T-shirt and slid to her hips and tugged her toward him. Sam fell into his warmth with a soft gasp as the hands that glided over piano keys so smoothly now played with her nipples. He pinched them with just enough pressure. "Tell me what would make you feel better. I'll give it to you," he said, right before sucking her nipple into his mouth along with the shirt.

A jolt of pleasure shot up her spine as his teeth tugged at the aching knot in a rough movement that made her core clench greedily. "Tell me where you would like my mouth so that..." One hand drifted down and snuck under her panties.

Sam closed her eyes as his fingers delved between her folds, played with her clit before the broad pad of his thumb notched into her opening. Dipping in and out, thrusting farther in with every motion while the pad of his palm pressed up against her clit... Her knees shook. Her entire body began that shuddering ascent, mindlessly in search of the freefall.

"Stay here with me, Sameera. Look at me. Kiss me," he demanded, as he always did when she was getting close. As if it was her vulnerability in that moment when she was tumbling, her greediness for whatever he gave her got him off. He always made her come when he was inside her even if it meant postponing his own release, even if that meant revving her all the way up again.

Fingers sinking into his hair, Sam almost climbed into his lap. But that arrogant possessiveness in his gaze arrested her. Bending, she scraped her teeth over his jaw roughly. His gravelly moan gave her a foothold to fight the need for her own pleasure.

Nope, today she wanted to own him. Today, she wanted to be the one that made him mindless. In this moment, she wanted her name on his lips, in his heart, vibrating through his entire being. Not the ghost of another woman.

It was nearly impossible to stop when release was a shimmering starburst one breath away, but she did it. Clasping his wrists, she went to her knees.

From this angle on the floor, he looked like some otherworldly god she could never hold on to. Could only have in flickers of finite moments. And those were dwindling faster and faster.

"Sam? What's going on in your head, *bella*?" A hint of frustration seeped into his words.

She lay a hand on the band of his sweatpants, her cheeks on fire. His abdomen clenched under her touch. A thrill shot through her at how sensitive he was, even to that simple contact. Licking her lips, she trailed her finger along the line of hair that thickened below his belly button and disappeared under his pants. "How come you never ask me to do this?"

Dark color crested his cheeks. His throat rippled, and Sam caught the flare of excitement in his eyes that he tried his best to suppress. And it lit a conflagration in her body. "Do what, *bella*?"

He was stalling until he could better control himself, she knew. "Go down on you."

His palms scraped along her forearm as he caught her mouth in a gentle kiss. "Because…we're still new to each other, *tesoro*."

"Yeah, but it's not like we have months for me to ease into it."

Their gazes held. All of time and space should have stilled around them. And yet, Sam could hear the laughter from the patio rise, the chitter of some insects, felt the cold marble floor against her knees, felt her heart go boom in her chest.

She slid her hand down his abdomen. His erection twitched in her palm, thick and hard. "I want to experience everything with you—"

"Tell me what has you so…perturbed."

She shook her head. "You're distracting me, and I won't be."

"*Bene*," he said, inclining his head. A king letting the peasant come to their knees.

He jerked his hips up, his sweatpants came down. Her breaths became a struggle as he took her palm and wrapped it around his shaft. A shuddering hiss filled her ears.

He was steel cloaked in velvet as she pumped up and

down slowly. Sensation fizzed around in her body, thrill and power and arousal colliding like fizzy bubbles.

His fingers pulled her hair away from her face, a dark humor in his eyes. "Open up, then, Sameera. Let's see what you can do today then, *si*?"

It was her turn to swallow.

His mouth curved into a sardonic twist. "Not time yet to swallow, *bella*."

"Don't mock me, Alessandro."

"I wouldn't dare."

Leaning forward, she licked the head where a bead of pre-cum glistened. He was salty and musky, and Sam went back for more. But for a breath before that, she looked up at him.

Head thrown back, the thick veins in his temple and neck stood out in stark relief. That didn't last for long, though.

As Sam continued to lap him up, up and down, over and under, his thighs turned granite under her fingers and his gaze locked down on her. As if seeing her do this was more arousing than the sensation of her mouth on him. Every new thing she tried, he let out a long growl, thrust his hips up as if he couldn't help himself.

Opening her mouth wide, Sam took as much as possible of him, and that wasn't much. His head barely touched her throat.

He cursed, long and filthy. "Slow down, *bella*. Breathe through it."

When she did it right, he went a little farther. In and out, she followed his command, hollowed her cheeks out, until the head hit the back of her throat. But he always pulled back before it became too much.

"You're such a good girl here, Sameera," he said, his words husky and gravelly. "If I had known you would submit so prettily to whatever filthy demands I make of you, I'd have made you go down on your knees the first time."

Sam looked up, eyes blazing, heart pumping fast, his taste an explosion on her tongue. "Well, now you know," she said catching a breath.

His grin was wicked, harsh, full of arrogant need. The floor at her knees was rough, his grip in her hair was rough, her mouth began to ache, but she had never felt more gloriously alive.

"*Basta*, Sameera!" he said, pulling out of her mouth.

"No, I want you to finish in my—"

Lifting her into his lap, Alessandro smiled against her mouth. She kissed him back sloppily, breath out of rhythm, cheeks aching, lips sensitized, but God, she wanted him to know how she felt. "Come in my mouth," she said with a pout. Between their bodies, his erection notched tightly against her belly.

He was shaking his head, tugging her to her feet. "Whatever you're trying to prove, Sam," he said, tightly clasping her face in his palms, "you don't have to. You're more than enough for me."

Words burst out of her. "Prove it, then."

A teasing glint appeared in his eyes as he played with her lower lip with the pad of his thumb. It was a gentling of sorts… "Prove it how, *bella*?"

"I don't know… I just want you mindless, like you make me."

"Come with me, then." A wicked glint shone in his eyes.

Sam followed him as he brought her to a vanity table.

New sensations skittered across her skin as he got her naked within seconds. His legs kicked hers out wider, and pockets of heat broke out all over.

While she watched their reflection in the mirror, he thrummed her all over. Her skin was flushed damp, she was panting and vibrating with need when he finally bent her over and stroked into her without hesitation and Sam had no rational thoughts left.

Everything on the vanity went flying as he slammed into her. "Look at me, Sameera," he whispered, his chest falling against her back. Watching her, moving through this moment with her. Binding her to him.

Sam looked in the mirror, and there he was. Dark and broad, eyes shot with lust, skin damp, desire etched into every pore. "See how mindless you make me, *bella*. See how I do not care that you're all swollen and puffed up down here. See how much I mark your tender flesh. See how desperate I am to come inside you, over and over."

A dark smile edged his lips. "You ruin me every time you let me do these things to you, Sam. And somehow you remake me too." His mouth came to her shoulder.

Sam braced herself, her core fluttering, clenching and releasing, around his thick length. But there was no escape from him, inside and out, and she didn't want that. Tingles raced down when he dug his teeth into her shoulder just as he stroked out and in.

Her body bowed, her legs shook, and her scream remained locked behind his rough fingers. He took her roughly, with barely any rhythm but a madness he was chasing, molding her body into what he needed.

As his thrusts became faster, his free palm moved from her chest to her clit. When climax broke her apart, when he groaned at his own release, when he picked her up and carried her to the tub and washed her body as if she were infinitely precious, Sam didn't have any thoughts or words left.

All she wanted was more days like these. More moments like this.

Her greedy heart wanted forever with the man who made her feel gloriously alive.

A few days had passed in a hazy, dreamy blur along with hot, steamy nights when Alessandro walked to Sam's studio on the second floor and stalled at the threshold.

For once, she wasn't at the easel, covered in paint like he usually found her. Found her and then distracted her whether she was done or not.

He'd had the room emptied and tidied because three walls were all-glass doors and the lighting in here was perfect. It had once been his mother's craft room, Papà had informed him. But he had no memory of her, neither did it hold any kind of sentimental value for him.

Now he could think of it as nothing but Sameera's studio. And when she left... The thought ran around in his head like a bullet ricocheting against the walls of an empty chamber, looking for a target.

But there was nothing to pin down, he reminded himself. He was able to feel this much, take all of what she gave because this was only a small pocket of time. If she were truly his for the rest of their lives, he didn't think he could survive the intensity of his feelings. Nor would she.

Months, or maybe years from now, the memories associated with this room, memories of Sam during this time, would simply fade. She'd become an interesting highlight in his past.

He knew why he was thinking such morose thoughts too. The banquet that was held for the cancer research foundation he'd established in Violetta's memory was tonight.

Though, tonight, he didn't want to think of the woman that had slipped away from his life. Tonight, as much as he couldn't skip the banquet, his mind constantly dwelled on Sam. As it had done since her arrival.

She was standing on the small balcony that the French doors led to. The smock she'd tied around her neck left her back bare except for the strap of her bra. The low-slung shorts hugged her bony hips and curvy ass, the only place she wasn't skinny, which she'd flashed and jiggled and rubbed up against him since she'd discovered it was his weakness, the cunning minx.

The shimmery orange of dusk's rays picked up the golden highlights in her hair, the result of a salon visit with Angelina.

Their friendship, as strangely as it had begun, didn't surprise Alessandro. For her youth—well, relative youth, he corrected in his head because she didn't like it when he called her *young*—Sam had an innate ability to empathize with people that made everyone like her.

Her elbows resting on the sill, she looked thoughtful.

"Sam?"

She turned and blinked, but he didn't miss the sheen of tears in her eyes.

"What's wrong?" he said, cutting the distance between them with long strides.

Leaning back against the balcony, she swept her gaze

over him, a tremulous smile coasting her lips. "Every time I think you couldn't be any sexier, you prove me wrong. You know what the tuxedo makes me want to do?"

"What, *bella*?" he asked, knowing that she was distracting him. It was a miracle that they'd managed to learn anything about each other at all. She was as secretive as he was. As stubborn as he.

"It makes me want to rumple you up. But then I think, nope the world can have this sophisticated version of you. The hungry, savage version is mine."

The raw, naked claiming both excited and tethered him, as always. "Give me a few hours and I'm all yours."

Reaching her, he pulled her until her back was against his chest and he wrapped his arms around her waist.

She fought a little first—a symptom of her clear upset, but he didn't relent.

It was strange how he was the one who had resisted touching her like this, outside of sex, and yet, now she was the one who fought any kind of tenderness or affection. Initially, he had worried that he had scared her with his unrestrained need at all hours. Nearly three weeks hadn't remotely dampened the intensity of his sexual hunger.

But no, she demanded release, she demanded every tender and filthy thing he could do to her, as insatiable as he was.

Still, something had made her spirit dim just a little, and he could not bear it. While he continued in the same vein outwardly, a quiet panic was beginning to build inside. That she was changing, that she was leaving soon. That she…

"Whatever it is that has been upsetting you these past few days," he said, holding her a little too tight, "we shall fix it, Sam. Together."

"How sweetly you make that offer, Mr. Ricci," she said, turning to look at him. Her fingers traced his lips while her gaze did the same to his features. "But we both know life doesn't bend to our whims. Not even to arrogant, powerful Italians whose kisses are pure sin."

He nudged his nose against the arch of her neck and shoulder, and finally she settled against him.

He loved holding her like this, as if he could capture her in this moment and space, as if he could control the tornado she was sweeping through his life. Even though it was nothing but an illusion.

He rested his chin in the crook of her neck and shoulder. "Please, Sam. Tell me what has upset you so."

"How come you didn't invite me to this charity banquet?" Her arm swept out between them, signaling to his formal attire. "Angelina told me all of Milan's high society will be there. Apparently, it's the social event of the year."

He rubbed a finger over his brow, his stomach strangely tight. "You wouldn't enjoy it."

She gave a slow nod, her eyes wide. "Is it that, or are you worried of what people will think when you bring me? You aren't ashamed of being seen with me, are you? Because I'm too young and naïve and fragile for your crowd?"

"That's the most ridiculous thing you've ever said to me." Ire coated his every word. He took a beat to breathe through the tight fist in his gut. "The evening is basically rich people showing off with their donations, courting me. And I do the whole song and dance because the charity means a lot to me. If you came," he said, his hesitation betraying him, "you would be bored by all the showboating."

"You like to keep me separate from the rest of the world, is that it?"

"*Sì*," he said with enough force that the calm around them fractured. "Is that so wrong? Is it wrong if I don't want the world to cast its eyes on you and speculate on our affair? You were distressed by it when it was just my family. I do not care what the entire damned world thinks of this thing between us, but you might be hurt. And I won't subject you to that."

"Okay," she said, running her hands over his collar, soothing him. Rubbing at a spot on his jacket with her finger. And then she gave up on the pretense and simply patted his chest with her palms.

He liked it when she touched him, but today it was different. Today there was a hesitation. As if she were gathering all of her courage to ask whatever it was. It filled him with tension. "Just ask, Sam. Whatever it is."

She looked up at him, surprise making her brown eyes impossibly wider. Then she sighed. "This banquet, the research foundation, it's all in her name, isn't it? Violetta."

He nodded. It was strange to hear Violetta's name on Sam's lips. But not as jarring as he'd imagined it would be. "How do you know?"

"One can't be your plaything and escape her name being thrown in one's face, Alessandro. But I want to know about her," she said, a wariness to her mouth. "Especially when it's clear that she was—*she is*—a big part of who you are." She swallowed slowly. "I mean, Angelina told me most of the details."

"What else is there to know?"

The sky was suddenly overcast, dark clouds rolling in. Like his mood.

Alessandro didn't know if he preferred the light or the dark for this conversation. Only that he didn't want to hurt Sam by saying the wrong thing. But stopping her when she set her mind to something was impossible. He'd learned that when he'd tried to stay away from her.

"I know that she fell sick a month after your engagement. That she endured a long fight with cancer. That you stayed by her side for four hellish years. That you—" She faced him then. Tears welled in her eyes, but she blinked them back. "I'm so sorry that you lost her, Alessandro."

Words escaped him as he beheld her. As she stared back at him, communicating all the pain she felt for him. For the future he'd lost. For the woman he'd loved as if she were his own breath. Acknowledgment of all he'd endured shimmered in her eyes. And yet it felt like benediction, not pity. Not comfort. Like acceptance without expectations that he move on, become normal again and be happy.

It felt like she was entering that space where he was most tormented and she was holding his hand through it. Telling him he wasn't alone.

Emotions whipped him around like a leaf in a storm. It shook him again how this woman was so fragile and yet so strong, so stubborn about venturing where she knew she'd be hurt and still plod along anyway because that's what life demanded.

"Then, you know everything, Sameera," he said, in that forbidding tone she teased him about but couldn't help.

"The thing is," she said, her breath an audible hitch, "everyone talks about how you lost her. How you changed after she was gone. How her death changed the very course of your life and I...hate that."

He felt as if one of Bruno's fists had connected with his solar plexus, punching his very breath out of him. Stunning him, tilting the axis of his life yet again.

"I want to know what kind of a woman she was. Tell me what made her angry, what made her laugh. Tell me about what...made you fall in love with her. Tell me about her."

"She was ambitious," Alessandro said, words rushing to his lips like a torrent unlocked. "She wanted to own the world as much as she wanted to change it. We were at school together. At eight or nine years old, she decided she wanted to be a doctor. She wanted to help people. She beat me at every competitive exam we took. She...called me on every bit of my arrogance." *Like you*, he didn't say. A laugh burst out of him. "She was the life of the party. She was petty about small things, could hold a grudge like no one else and was generous where it mattered."

"She sounds lovely," Sam said, and he could tell it wasn't a platitude.

"She was," Alessandro said, as sudden darkness completely blanketed them.

Sameera shivered, and he gathered her to him, although it was for his own comfort. He swept his palms all over her—the bare midriff, the toned arms, the silky skin—and as he warmed her up, he told her all about Violetta.

He talked about things even he'd forgotten. Things he'd buried so far deep in his heart that they had ceased to exist. Everything Violetta once had been came roaring back to life in his words. Wrenched forth by this woman who was made of sunlight and laughter. It was as if Sam had reintroduced Violetta back to him as something more than a dying woman.

When it got too cold, when his chest felt so light as if someone had shifted a heavy weight from his shoulders, he swept Sam into his arms and brought her inside.

Moonlight rendered her exquisite for him, just for him. He sat with her in his lap on the chaise, and he kissed her, the moment as fragile and tenuous as the joy in his heart.

And despite the fact that he was about to break his own rules, he made love to her. Uncaring that he was late. Uncaring that he'd look less than perfect. Uncaring that she had become a weakness that could and would shatter him soon.

He stripped her of every inch of clothing and hugged her trembling, silky form to him, pretending that she needed him as much as he did her.

He worshipped her with his mouth, his fingers, with everything in him. He wrenched an orgasm out of her, swallowing her cries and mewls, before he buried himself deep inside her. He drove into her like a possessed man seeking freedom, uncaring of her fragility.

The dark amplified her groans and his hunger. And yet, it was slow and lazy and soft when his own orgasm broke, a balm to his shattered heart.

He wrapped her up in a blanket and lay down with her on the chaise longue until she fell asleep. And then he kissed her temple, traced that scar that he knew better than his own hand now, listened to the steady beat of her heart and left for the banquet.

It wasn't until hours later that Alessandro noticed a drop of dark red paint on the lapels of his pristine dress shirt. A bright pink streak on his neck. A yellow dot on his chest. She'd done it on purpose, he knew.

Rumpled him up. Splashed color onto the empty canvas of his life. Changed him, made him hers, even if for just a little.

He liked it. And for the first time in fifteen years, his heart didn't feel heavy at the thought of Violetta.

For Sam had helped him remember all the glorious things about her. All the stubborn things. And more than anything, she'd helped him remember that Violetta had loved life. To the last moment. And that he wanted that for himself too.

Sam woke alone a few hours later, her skin cold, her limbs sort of frozen, and pulled the blanket Alessandro had wrapped around her tighter.

When she stretched her legs tentatively on the chaise longue, her core ached, instantly reminding her of how possessively he had taken her before he had left.

How reverentially he had kissed every inch of her skin. How his fingers had left brief divots in her flesh.

Her body ached and throbbed while her heart, her foolish heart, soared at yet another new experience. Uncaring of the crash it had signed up for.

She had fallen in love with him, with the man whose heart would always belong to a dead woman. She knew it as well as the stuttered beat of her heart, her warm breath and her aching body. Knew that this trip, this adventure that she had so desperately wanted, had changed her. Irrevocably. More than anything ever could.

She also knew that she could not share this vast, brilliant truth with him, that Alessandro wouldn't want it. That she wasn't strong enough to face his gentle, polite but irrefutable rejection of her love. That she couldn't bear to compete with Violetta's memories.

She deserved better. She deserved him, fully, wholly, unconditionally. She deserved that deep, vast, kind heart of his that could feel so much.

Sighing, she untangled herself from the chaise and got to her feet. Her knees quaked, and a sob surged up through her chest, nearly breaking her. God, she loved him so much and she always would. One look at her and he would know, and the one thing she couldn't bear to see was his pity.

He'd given her the taste of an entire lifetime in a few weeks, and that had to be enough.

She was gone.

Alessandro had known it even as he'd walked up the steps into the house, returning in the early hours of the morning after the charity banquet.

As strange as it sounded, he'd felt it from the moment he'd stepped out of the car in the courtyard and knew it with a certainty even before he reached the bedroom.

Their bedroom...

It was free of all the hundred things she'd scattered about. Now it looked sterile and empty, like a damned coffin for all he could breathe in there.

She'd left without good-bye. She'd left before her vacation was up. There was at least another week left. He knew, because he'd been counting the days like a lovesick fool.

He rushed to the studio, and that was as empty as his heart.

Matteo found him in the studio, the creek of the elevator doors and his wheelchair alerting Alessandro.

"She didn't discuss this with you?" Uncharacteristic gravity filled his brother's voice.

Alessandro shook his head. He doubted if he could form words even if he tried. His chest felt like it was collapsing on itself, an ocean of pain drowning him.

He'd imagined how it would feel once she left. He'd prepared himself for the sudden emptiness, for that stark silence of his life again. He'd get used to it, he told himself. He'd pick the pieces of his life back up again, like people did after a storm blew over.

But the reality was so much worse. Everything in him felt blank, silent, oppressively empty. As if she'd taken all of him with her. Given him back his ability to feel, such searing joy and crushing sorrow, and then taken it back.

The alternative was unthinkable. If he pursued a future with her, if he even indulged in the idea of it and then lost her…the pain would be unbearable. Worse than when he'd lost Violetta.

Because despite everything, he had barely been on the cusp of manhood when he'd lost her. He hadn't known himself fully before he had become part of a couple, only to lose her. He'd been angry, resentful that the world didn't bend and sway at his command, and he'd simply shut himself off.

This thing he felt for Sam…it defied definition. Refused to be caged into words. The love he felt in his heart was all encompassing, so vast that it turned all his assumptions into dust. It humbled him, restored his faith in everything around him.

Losing her was worse than any pain he had imagined from loving her and living with the fear that her heart might give out. Much worse.

But what did she feel for him?

Doubts unlike he'd ever known engulfed him.

Had it been easy for her to leave without saying goodbye? Had he truly been nothing but a part of her summer adventure?

"She said something's up with her parents and she needed to be there. She also said...she did what she came to prove, to herself and her parents. That she was ready to leave, Alessandro. Nothing could've stopped her. She asked me if I could book her on an immediate flight. I didn't know she hadn't..."

Alessandro flicked a glance at his brother.

Whatever Matteo saw there, he swallowed and looked away. He wheeled closer to Alessandro. If not for the fact that his heart was shattering in his chest, Alessandro would've laughed at the role reversal.

His brother, it seemed, really had grown up. For he didn't offer platitudes or suggestions. He simply stayed there in the darkness and kept him company as Alessandro fell apart silently.

He wanted that joy of laughing with her again, that glorious feeling of being alive when they fought, that sense of purpose he found when she let him look after her, that soul-deep connection when he slid into her welcoming heat.

He buried his head in his hands, feeling a desolation unlike he'd ever tasted.

How would he have borne seeing her walk away from him? How would he have felt knowing that she was moving on with her adventures, with her life, while he stayed stuck, standing still without her by his side?

Could he love her without suffocating her with his own fears? Without stifling her glorious spirit? Without making his love a shackle?

He wanted to love her for the rest of his life. And that meant being the bravest version of himself. For the woman he loved had the most courageous heart, and he wanted to be its equal.

CHAPTER TWELVE

Six weeks later

SAM THREW HER backpack under the console table in the small foyer of her parents' house and kicked off her single sneaker with unwarranted violence.

Which made the grocery bag in her arms shake in her grasp. The salad she'd picked up at the deli fell to the tiled floor with a quiet thud. Which meant there was now lettuce and carrots and grape tomatoes scattered all over the floor with the dressing splattered and staring back at her. Which also meant her dad would have to clean it up because Sam couldn't bend her left leg right now.

Sudden, indulgent tears filled her eyes, and she pressed her forehead to the door.

Her right hip ached with how much extra load she'd been putting on it to compensate for the giant bruise on her left hip. God forbid she be of use to anyone else. For once in her life, she wanted to be the one who didn't need looking after.

But it wasn't just the frustration of the accident she'd had since returning or the anger over how exhausted she was by the end of the week after juggling classes, her portrait commissions and schlepping home every evening from the campus.

It was *him*.

She wasn't sleeping because she missed him in her bed. Missed being held by him. Missed his gaze on her, relentlessly digging and probing. Missed the warm curve of his mouth as he pressed it to her skin.

She wasn't enjoying her college experience because everything felt colorless without him.

She had no appetite, but she forced herself to eat anyway because that's what grown-up people did. Even when their heart was torn into pieces. Especially grown-up Sam because her damned heart couldn't be trusted to not fail on her if she didn't look after herself.

Just another week before she was free of the cast on her foot, she reminded herself.

This too shall pass, she repeated to herself, as if her life depended on it.

She'd wanted adventures and life, and that meant heartbreak too.

Apparently real life for her meant falling in love with the wrong brother in a matter of a few weeks and running away without even telling him how she truly felt because she was terrified of seeing his irrefutable rejection of her love.

But she'd get over him, as she did with all hard things in life, and be stronger for it. Just not yet. It would take her all of her twenties probably. Maybe some of her thirties.

By thirty-five, she'd be ready to throw herself into another red-hot affair. And maybe she would target a man from a different continent this time, just for variety.

That ridiculous plan for the next decade felt like control when nothing else was in her grasp.

Stepping around the wilting lettuce and sodden carrots, she walked into the house, only noticing then that it was too quiet for a Friday evening.

Her mom's favorite Indian soap opera—hers too, now—should've been playing loud enough to drive Dad bonkers. The thought broke her dark mood. Even her dad's old excuse that he didn't understand Hindi didn't stand anymore. In the vein of all soap operas across the universe, the show moved so slowly and so dramatically that even he could understand what was happening.

"Mom, what's happening? Did Rishika discover the truth about her evil twin? Has she—"

Her breath emptied out of her in a loud, long exhale.

Alessandro was standing in their kitchen, a bottle of her dad's favorite beer dripping condensation all over the granite counter next to him.

White dress shirt and black trousers. His hair needed a cut. His mouth was set in that tight, forbidding line she knew so well. And his eyes… God, his eyes. A rainbow of emotions flickered through them as they roved over her hungrily.

From her hair in two braids to the Band-Aid on her chin to her crop top and low-slung shorts to the large blue-green bruise showing on her hip and her foot in a cast.

His gaze lingered at several points, mainly her foot and the bruise, and then crawled up to her face. Tension thrummed around him, as if he were creating a strange force field around himself.

He should have looked so out of context here in their

kitchen, in their house. At least that's how she'd survived the last few weeks. By compartmentalizing him in her head, like a fantasy. A temporary illusion that had felt incredibly good.

In silence, she walked into the living room where her parents were on the couch, and Alessandro followed. On the big plasma screen on the wall, Rishika was running around the streets of Mumbai chasing after her amnesiac lover who was being stolen away by her evil twin.

Sam registered this on the periphery of her senses, as if they were a background track for her suddenly very vivid life. Someone muted the television.

Her mom finally broke the silence. "Why didn't you tell us you were dating Matteo's older brother?"

Sam's eyes widened. He'd told them? What, exactly?

"For God's sake, Sameera, he's eighteen years older than you. I can't decide if he's worse than Matteo or not. Because *he* should know better." This she addressed to Alessandro with an almighty scowl.

Heat rushed into her cheeks, but Sam couldn't break away from that gray gaze. Dad's *Hush, Geeta, let them sort it out* fell into the tense silence.

Alessandro raised an eyebrow.

Fluent in his facial language, Sam understood him instantly.

He was asking whether she wanted him to answer her mom's inquiries.

The gesture was so familiar, had haunted her so much, that raw longing flooded her body. For a wild, crazy moment, she wanted to say *Go for it*. She wanted to let him take on her mom and see the fireworks. She wanted to see what he'd say about them now that they were... Wait, why was he here at all?

"Sam?"

She turned to her mom, hearing the worry in it. "Whatever it was, it's over now, Mom." She heard the catch of pain in her voice but had no energy to fight it. "So let's not argue about the irrefutable fact that I'm an adult, and while you're allowed to express your opinion, you have no say in how I live my life, hmm?"

"Then, why is he here?" her mom continued. "He's been here all afternoon and grilled us about you for hours."

Her belly swooped. He'd been waiting all afternoon?

She turned to Alessandro. "Are you going to just stand there and look at me, or explain why you're here?" she said, her stomach twisting. Did he have any idea how hard it was for her to see him here like this and not touch him? To fight being pulled back into his gravity? "If not, Mom will continue to talk about you as if you're not standing there taking up all the space." Sudden anxiety flooded her. "Wait, is Matteo okay? Angelina didn't say anything about—"

"Matteo is fine."

No one could have missed the jealousy in his tone. *No one.* Sam blinked.

"Are you in pain?" he asked, tilting his chin at her foot.

"It's just a hairline fracture," she said, clumsily wiggling her foot.

That he'd ask her that of all the hundred things he could've said...her heart felt like a fragile piece of glass. Liable to shatter at one wrong word. And because she would hate him to reach the wrong conclusion, she elaborated. "This…teen kid was driving a moped and almost crashed into a delivery vehicle. I tried to get him out of his way, right outside. I ended up twisting my foot and falling," she finished slowly.

He didn't nod at her explanation. His gaze didn't relent, as if his intensity had been dialed to the max. "Pack a bag. We'll go to my hotel suite." He rubbed a hand over his temple. "Do you need help?"

Her mom's outraged gasp punctured the silence. God, she couldn't give them a moment, could she? And what was Alessandro doing, ordering her around, in front of her parents?

Despite it all, Sam was tempted. Beyond tempted to simply follow him.

He could have said they'd go to the end of earth or a different dimension or a parallel universe and she'd still have followed him. If he'd asked for a few more weeks, or days or even one last night for closure…she'd be all in. Again. She'd put aside embarrassment, her self-respect, her pain—everything if he'd just kiss her one more time. If he'd hold her. If he'd make love to her. She was that desperate for him.

But if she did go, she wasn't sure she could break away again. The thought of his rejection was the slap of common sense she needed.

"I have an early morning class, and it's my turn to make dinner tonight," she said, uncaring that it sounded like an excuse. It wasn't.

He came toward her. A strange dizziness came over her as he took the bag of groceries in one hand, grabbed her waist with the other and simply lifted her and carried her to the kitchen.

Sam breathed him in like an addict.

"I will help with dinner. We can eat and then go. I'll make sure you get to class on time in the morning."

Sam simply nodded instead of telling him she was not going anywhere with him.

To his credit, he did help her in the kitchen. But her heart couldn't simply settle down in his proximity.

Since she'd lost the salad, she heated up leftover rice and used the vegetables he'd chopped to make fried rice.

Her parents watched from the living room as if two aliens had taken over the kitchen.

Sam set the table while Alessandro scrambled the eggs until they were golden and fluffy and just…perfect like everything he did. It was such a domestic yet extraordinary moment that she didn't know what to think.

"I didn't know you could cook," Sam said, when the four of them settled down around the table.

"You don't know a lot of things about me," he said, a soft twinkle in his eyes. "You ran away before I could tell you." The last part was a whisper just for her ears.

"I didn't run away," Sam retorted.

He didn't argue back, but the tight set of his jaw said more than enough.

If the fried rice was too spicy for him, he didn't let on. He ate two helpings as if it was the most delicious dish he'd ever tried, and a fierce kind of joy stabbed through Sam's middle.

Mom stayed quiet, but Dad and Alessandro chatted about computers and business and the Ricci branch in California without an ounce of awkwardness.

Soon they'd piled up all the dishes around the sink and she'd cleaned the dining table. Her heart started rabbiting in her chest.

"I'll see to these," Dad said, gesturing to the dirty dishes while Mom filled the kettle and turned it on. Sam didn't know what to do with herself. Or the sudden tremors that seemed to overtake her at the thought of him leaving.

Alessandro thanked her parents for their hospitality and did it with such genuine regard that even her mom cracked a smile. Then he turned to her. "Ready to go?"

Sam followed him into the living room so that they could have some privacy. Not so much that she'd lose the little sense of self-preservation that was holding her back. "I'm...exhausted, to be honest. It's been a long week."

He crowded her until their chests grazed. "I can see that, *tesoro*. You can just sleep. We don't have to talk." His knuckles traced the dark shadows under her eyes. "I just...need to hold you."

Sam stared, in shock. She hadn't imagined the slight catch in his tone. Hadn't imagined the bob of his Adam's apple. He sounded on edge. Stepping back, she looked up into his face, and something slid into place. "Wait, did Angelina tell you about my accident?"

"Does it matter, Sam?"

"Yes, it does," she said, her voice rising, aware that her parents were staring at them. "Where's your blasted honesty now?"

"Fine," he said with that infuriating calm in the face of her temper. "She was at the house yesterday. She mentioned that you had a short stay in the hospital two weeks ago. I flew here overnight."

She felt as if she'd been punched in the gut. Pushing away from him, she'd have stumbled if not for the wall at her back. "Did you come because you thought I was dying?" Tears pricked, never far these days. "As you can see, I'm perfectly fine, and you can fuck off with your pity. I don't have—"

She never finished. Because the blasted man picked her up in his arms all the while being extremely gentle with her foot and walked up the stairs.

Sam buried her face in his chest but didn't protest. Or fight. Or say anything. She was too busy crying, falling apart, to put up a fight. And it felt like her heart was breaking all over again.

To leave him once had been heartbreaking, but to do it again…she wasn't strong enough.

Alessandro deposited Sam onto the small bed in the attic room. While every cell in him wanted to crowd her into the bed, kiss her and generally railroad her into submission, he backed off. This wasn't a small thing, and the last thing he wanted was to restart their relationship with him minimizing her complaints.

He looked around the small room. Pictures of Sam greeted him from a bulletinboard, from all ages and sizes. Framed art hung from the wall, some her own pieces and some not. Her room was a kaleidoscope of colors and sunlight and shimmer. Just like her.

Seeing a familiar face on the board, he went closer for a better look. It was a picture of Matteo and Sam with his arm around her, younger and grinning into the camera.

He backed away, that prick of jealousy as fresh as always. But before he turned, one last thing caught his attention. It was a sketch of him, rendered in nothing but dark lines. That dark void that had opened up within him since she'd left ate it up hungrily.

Finally, he turned to find Sam glaring at him, her face etched with exhaustion. "Go to sleep, *bella*. You clearly need..." He swallowed the rest.

"As soon as you leave."

"I'm not leaving, Sameera. Not until we talk. It's not too late to go to the hotel. We'll have privacy and more room," he said, eyeing the single bed. There was no way he could sleep next to her on that.

"There's nothing I want to do with you that requires privacy."

He crawled onto her small bed, nuzzled into her temple and whispered, "I do."

She sniffled, and a tear made a track down her cheek. He wiped it away with his sleeve. "That's gross. I have tissues," she said.

"I've licked things off of your body, *tesoro*. This is nothing."

Pink crested her cheeks, and a tentative smile curved her mouth. When he reached for her hand, she gave it reluctantly. He laced his fingers through hers, and something in his chest settled. Like a key sliding into place, turning tumblers, unlocking a whole new world of joy and contentment for him.

It had started turning from the first moment. He'd been too numb inside to see it happening, to appreciate it.

"Why did you leave without saying good-bye?"

"My cousin Kavi...remember her?"

"The one that called you a stubborn goat? *Sì*. I like her."

He felt her surprise rather than saw it. Did she think

he'd forgotten a single moment of the time they'd spent together?

"She finally told me what was happening here. She always tells it like it is. Mom and Dad...are pregnant. That's what set her off to a near breakdown. She...she's forty-six, and she was terrified the baby might have the same genetic heart condition I have. They were doing all these tests to see if it was even viable. Her blood pressure was out of control. A little baby brother... Can you imagine?"

Fresh tears filled her eyes, and he tucked her face into his shoulder.

Relief made him shudder when she stayed there. "Anyway, they're having this baby, and I told them I'd cut them off completely if they kept secrets from me ever again. Or if they treated me like a child anymore. I love the idea of him so much already, Alessandro. I think I understand some of her overprotectiveness with me."

"She and the baby are healthy?"

"Everything's good. Perfect." She pulled back to look into his face. "After Kavi told me, I wanted to be here for them. But of course I had an accident not two weeks after coming back."

"I'm sorry you were hurt, *tesoro*."

"That's not the point."

"What is?"

"I wanted to look after her. Not the other way around."

"But this is just an unfortunate accident, and you saved a kid from getting hurt worse. It's got nothing to do with your abilities." He lifted her knuckles to his mouth and kissed them. "As for looking after you...why do you automatically assume that it's a burden? It's abundantly clear how much she loves you." He gentled his tone. "You didn't tell me she's a lawyer. She grilled me for hours today. It's natural that she…worries about you. It doesn't mean she doesn't think you capable, Sameera." With a bracing breath, he added, "Some people have a hard time dealing with boundaries when they love someone. You say you understand her need to protect you a little now? Then, give her some grace, *no*?"

Sam stared at him. She'd been at odds with her parents ever since she'd returned, even though they'd finally gotten their act together. But one look at her face and Alessandro seemed to understand exactly what she needed to hear. It was why he'd helped with dinner too. Because he understood it was important to her.

"Why didn't you at least call me?" he said.

There was something in his words that tugged at her, but she was too exhausted to figure it out. Neither could she manage flippancy. "You know I hate confrontations."

He tensed. "Good-bye would have been a confrontation?"

"Yes, because I couldn't have stopped blurting out that I'm in love with you. And you'd have given me a hundred reasons for why we don't suit, super politely and then—"

Sam squealed as in a blink he'd flipped her onto the bed and covered her body with his. The delicious weight of him pressing down made her eyes roll back. His mouth hovered over hers, his gray eyes roiling with such emotion that it made her chest ache. "I wish you'd stayed and confronted me. Then I'd have told you I'm in love with you too, and then it wouldn't have felt like my heart had been trampled when I found you gone."

Sam wondered if her heart might jump out of her chest. Tears gathered in her throat and trickled down her eyes onto the bed. "I…"

Shifting to his side, he pressed his face into her neck, one hand palming her all over. "I rushed here after Angelina told me, *sì*. But I'd have been here anyway in a couple of weeks, *bella*. Some of the arrangements were taking time. Especially with Matteo still in recovery and my father grumbling about coming out of retirement."

"What arrangements?" Sam finally whispered.

Her chest still felt too full of wonder and disbelief. Too vulnerable about this sudden happiness. She couldn't believe he was saying these words to her. That he was here, touching her, kissing her and looking at her as if she meant everything to him. It was the stuff of her wildest dreams.

"Moving headquarters from Milan to California is quite an upheaval."

"You're moving to Cali? Why?"

"I want to be near you."

A vast ocean of happiness opened up in her, sucking her in. "Why?"

Gray eyes held hers, but this time Sam needed words. And he seemed to know that. He kissed the corner of her mouth, rubbed the tip of his nose against hers, as if he needed to brace himself to say them. "Because my life is colorless without you, *tesoro*. It is unbearable. Every morning, every evening, every moment in between…it's empty. And because I'm an arrogant asshole, it took me too long to realize that my happiness is a choice I have to make. That it lies with you."

Sam tried to smile but more tears rolled down her cheeks.

"I'm not going anywhere, Sam," Alessandro said, kissing her with such reverent tenderness that she wanted to burrow into him. His hands traced the seam of her top, careful to not touch the bruise on her hip. "I know that you have all these plans for your new colorful life, like college and raves and... I just ask that you let me be a part of your life. Even if all you can give me are weekends and—"

"So you want to be my weekend boyfriend? Am I allowed to date other men during weekdays?"

"I was hoping you'd agree to the exclusive thing again," he said oh so politely, as if his gray eyes weren't full of a stormy bleakness. "All I want is to love you, Sameera. To show you how much you mean to me."

"I...but you love Violetta. I can't—won't share you with anyone, Alessandro. Not even the past."

He didn't mock her or talk down to her. A harsh sigh left him. "I understand the feeling. Every time you mention Matteo with that affection, I want to break his pretty face." He shook his head. "A part of me will always love Violetta, *sì*. But that's a tiny part, Sam. Until you made me talk about her, it wasn't even her I remembered. It was the pain, the loss and the powerlessness of losing her. She became nothing but a reason I used to shut myself off. You..."

His breath rattled and his voice broke, and it was long moments before he spoke again. "You are laughter and joy and pleasure and fragility and innocence and stubbornness and fear and... I want to spend the rest of my life loving you, kissing you, laughing with you, playing chess with you, fighting with you…" He rubbed at her top where the scar lay, and Sam knew he wasn't even aware of it. That it had taken him everything to fight the fear of losing her. "That I feel this much for you, it scares me. The *what-if*s that go around in my head… But I won't be a coward anymore. I won't deny myself this chance with you. Not a day, not a moment. This happiness…it's a choice I'm making, even though it terrifies me, Sam."

"You do know that I can't have children, right? And that my life will—"

His hand covered her mouth. "I was a shadow, living a half life until you blazed into it, filled it with colors and emotions again. All I want is a future with you, whatever its shape, *tesoro*. Please, don't doubt my faith in this, in us."

Sam grabbed his hand and pressed a kiss to the center of his palm. "I've been hurting all over," she said, wanting to bask in their closeness, "so make me feel better, Alessandro. Give me all of you," she demanded, pushing up on elbows to press her mouth to his.

He didn't need to be asked again. Whispering her name as if it were a benediction, Alessandro kissed her with such tenderness that Sam felt like her heart was coming back to life again. Her bed was tiny for his frame, but she loved that because it gave him no room to move away from her.

He trailed kisses down her cheek to her neck, and before she knew it, her top was gone and his lips left blistering warmth all over her breasts and her midriff. There was no inch of her that he didn't touch or kiss or nip. And yet all of that frenzy calmed down in a matter of breaths as his fingers tugged at the seam of her shorts.

"I hate seeing these bruises on your body," he said, and then let out a curse. "Don't be mad, Sam." Slowly, softly, he kissed the perimeter of the blue-green bruise. "I told myself I would not stifle you or suffocate you or make you think you're incapable. I just… The thought of you in pain or anything happening to you…turns me inside out."

Sam buried her fingers in his hair and tugged until he looked up at her. The naked love in his eyes made her hiccup like a child, as if he were a fantasy that might disappear the moment she opened her eyes. "It's okay. I want to know these things you feel. And you're already doing better."

And then she was naked, and he was kissing her all over, his fingers pulling and tugging, and she was like those piano keys he played so deftly. One more breath and she'd fall away and…

"My parents," Sam exclaimed and then giggled. She cast a look around the room and groaned. "Every little sound carries down from this room. I don't think I can ever face them again."

Alessandro nipped at her right hip, hard enough to leave a small mark on her skin. "Will you listen to me next time when I say we need privacy?"

"*Sì*. Absolutely."

He grinned and buried his mouth in her inner thigh. Another nip at the silky flesh, revving her up all over again. "Didn't you hear them? Their car left a while ago."

"What?"

Alessandro rubbed her lower lip as if he couldn't stop touching her. "I spoke to your dad earlier when your mom took a nap. I wasn't sure if you'd…" He flicked her nose.

"I wanted you all to myself tonight. I told him there's a room in their name at the Four Seasons in case he wanted to take your mom out for the night, and in case you refused to come to the hotel with me. I wanted all bases covered to have you to myself."

Sam bit her lower lip, but the smile broke through anyway. "I'm not going to encourage you going behind my back and conspiring with my parents of all people... but in this case, I excuse you. I guess my dad likes you."

Alessandro grinned. "And he knows you better than your mom does." That wide, wonky smile winked at her. The change in him—the sheer happiness in his expression was like a balm to her heart. She did want his words, but nothing spoke more eloquently than his gray eyes.

"Although, I'd prefer to not talk about him right now."

In reply, Sam snuck her hands in between them until she could wrap her palm around his erection. "Come inside me, please," she said, cheeks heating at the length and feel of him. Her core clenched, greedy and damp. "I won't break, Alessandro, not because of a couple of bruises and a broken foot. And that's the only way this relationship will work."

He opened his mouth, shook his head and then closed it. She laughed.

Between kisses and laughter, somehow, they managed to push his pants down, and then he was notched at her entrance. Then there was no reason for words.

He thrust into her, slowly, softly, stretching her impossibly wide, whispering so many words she didn't understand into her skin. And when he was lodged all the way in, he told her how she felt, how he'd been thinking of this moment, how he'd never stop wanting her.

Sex with him had always been a study in vulnerability and boundaries and falling off the edge when those boundaries were crossed. But this time, it was different. Their hands clasped, their eyes holding each other, joy suffused every movement, every word.

The blasted man took his own sweet time. And when Sam begged him to let her come, he tilted their angle and went deeper and faster, and she unraveled. Even their climaxes felt different, felt so much more than simple release. When he'd have pulled away, Sam held him, loving the weight of him on her and said the words she knew he wanted to hear. "I love you, Alessandro. You make me want to take risks, you make me come alive, and you…"

He took over and kissed her and whispered more words in Italian, and Sam knew she had found her grand adventure and her resting place all in one man.

It was dark in the room when Sam woke.

She turned to find Alessandro leaning his head on his elbow, studying her, his fingers drawing lazy circles over her belly. She flushed as she realized he'd not only cleaned her up but dressed her back in her shorts. "I didn't mean to fall asleep."

"I like looking after you." He grinned, something wicked and naughty flaring in his eyes. "Plus, I know how much you dislike being all sticky."

She flushed, heat rushing to her cheeks.

"I love when you get that expression in your eyes, *tesoro*. Reminds me there's so much more we still have to do with each other. To each other."

Moving onto her side, she faced him. With him around, she needed to get used to feeling warm and gooey and wanted and satisfied. A state of being she liked very much.

She didn't miss the thoughtful look in his eyes or the tension that drew his upper lip into that taut line before he covered it up with a grin. And Sam had a niggle what had put that look in his eyes.

She ran her hand over his chest, adoring the feeling of his skin stretched taut over lean muscles. He was hers. It was going to take time to get used to it. He was also a man who felt deeply, a man who suppressed every need and desire he felt first.

Sam wanted to be what he needed. Give what he wouldn't demand. "If I ask you something, will you give me an honest answer?" she said, unable to hide the gravity in her voice.

His gaze flicked to hers. "Ask me."

"I can't tell you how much I appreciate you moving to California. Because I can't leave Mom and Dad right now. I want to be here when the baby comes. But after… when things have settled down, we can go back to Italy, if you want. I know you're leaving at a hard time for your family too."

"I made these plans before I knew about the baby or your accident, Sam. I want to be where you are."

She nodded, her heart bursting to full. She pressed her mouth to his chest, the thundering din of his heart soothing her. "Will you tell me what is truly in your heart? What do you want from this?"

He gathered her to him and buried his face in her hair. Hiding the vulnerability he felt, she knew. When he spoke, his voice was hoarse. "I promised myself that I won't railroad you. That I'll let you choose the shape of our future. You have all these dreams and plans, and I don't want to take over your life and...your mom's complaint that I'm too old for you...it's not unfair."

"Not the answer to my question."

He looked at her, and those gray eyes captivated her. And that she had the power to grant all the wants in them was a trip of its own.

"I would marry you tomorrow. I would wrap you in Bubble Wrap and steal you away to my bedroom. I would..."

A soft gasp escaped her. He pressed a hand to his eyes, and shook his head. "I knew it was a bad idea."

"No. Listen, Alessandro. I... What about one out of the two?"

His head jerked up. "What?"

"The first one...the marrying part."

"But you want to go to college and—"

"And I can't if we marry?" Sam clasped his jaw and willed him to believe her. "Before I met you... I wanted what I thought was a normal life. College and parties and raves and dating...all the stuff I missed out on. But I hate parties, and the whole idea of dating terrifies me, and I wouldn't touch anything at a rave. I think men in their twenties are mostly immature." She clasped his cheeks, her heart overflowing with love. "Everything fades into gray scale when I think of my life without you. You're my grand adventure. My excitement. The one man who sees me...all of me. College and painting and building my own business... I can still do all of them with you in my life, *si*? We will just fight as husband and wife instead."

He laughed, kissed her, swirling his tongue against

hers with a possessive urgency. "Then, marry me tomorrow. Be my wife. Give me all of you."

Sam burrowed into him, her mouth at the hollow of his throat, her heart running away. "You have all of me, Alessandro. And yes, I'll marry you. As soon as you can arrange it."

Sam cried again, and Alessandro gathered her to him, and they fell asleep like that, all tangled in each other, waiting for the new dawn that would tie them together forever.

* * * * *

Were you blown away by
Italian's Last-Minute Mistress?
Then why not explore these other dazzling stories by Tara Pammi?

Contractually Wed
Her Twin Secret
Vows to a King
His Forgotten Wife
Baby Before Vows

Available now!

Get up to 4 Free Books!

We'll send you 2 free books from each series you try PLUS a free Mystery Gift.

Both the **Harlequin Presents** and **Harlequin Medical Romance** series feature exciting stories of passion and drama.

YES! Please send me 2 FREE novels from Harlequin Presents or Harlequin Medical Romance and my FREE gift (gift is worth about $10 retail). After receiving them, if I don't wish to receive any more books, I can return the shipping statement marked "cancel." If I don't cancel, I will receive 6 brand-new larger-print novels every month and be billed just $7.19 each in the U.S., or $7.99 each in Canada, or 4 brand-new Harlequin Medical Romance Larger-Print books every month and be billed just $7.19 each in the U.S. or $7.99 each in Canada, a savings of 20% off the cover price. It's quite a bargain! Shipping and handling is just 50¢ per book in the U.S. and $1.25 per book in Canada.* I understand that accepting the 2 free books and gift places me under no obligation to buy anything. I can always return a shipment and cancel at any time. The free books and gift are mine to keep no matter what I decide.

Choose one: ☐ **Harlequin Presents Larger-Print** (176/376 BPA G36Y)   ☐ **Harlequin Medical Romance** (171/371 BPA G36Y)   ☐ **Or Try Both!** (176/376 & 171/371 BPA G36Z)

Name (please print)

Address   Apt. #

City   State/Province   Zip/Postal Code

Email: Please check this box ☐ if you would like to receive newsletters and promotional emails from Harlequin Enterprises ULC and its affiliates. You can unsubscribe anytime.

Mail to the **Harlequin Reader Service:**
IN U.S.A.: P.O. Box 1341, Buffalo, NY 14240-8531
IN CANADA: P.O. Box 603, Fort Erie, Ontario L2A 5X3

Want to explore our other series or interested in ebooks? Visit www.ReaderService.com or call 1-800-873-8635.

---

*Terms and prices subject to change without notice. Prices do not include sales taxes, which will be charged (if applicable) based on your state or country of residence. Canadian residents will be charged applicable taxes. Offer not valid in Quebec. This offer is limited to one order per household. Books received may not be as shown. Not valid for current subscribers to the Harlequin Presents or Harlequin Medical Romance series. All orders subject to approval. Credit or debit balances in a customer's account(s) may be offset by any other outstanding balance owed by or to the customer. Please allow 4 to 6 weeks for delivery. Offer available while quantities last.

Your Privacy—Your information is being collected by Harlequin Enterprises ULC, operating as Harlequin Reader Service. For a complete summary of the information we collect, how we use this information and to whom it is disclosed, please visit our privacy notice located at https://corporate.harlequin.com/privacy-notice. Notice to California Residents – Under California law, you have specific rights to control and access your data. For more information on these rights and how to exercise them, visit https://corporate.harlequin.com/california-privacy. For additional information for residents of other U.S. states that provide their residents with certain rights with respect to personal data, visit https://corporate.harlequin.com/other-state-residents-privacy-rights/.